Slices of Life

For Paddy & Regina,
With love.
Pan –

Also by Patrick Semple

A Parish Adult Education Handbook – Editor

Believe It Or Not – A Memoir

That Could Never Be – with K Dalton

The Rectory Dog – Poetry Collection

The Rector Who Wouldn't Pray For Rain – A Memoir

A Narrow Escape – Poetry Collection

Transient Beings – A Novel

Curious Cargo – A Travelogue

Being Published – A Creative Writing Guide

Slices of Life

Patrick Semple

A collection of short stories

Code Green Publishing

ISBN 978-1-907215-22-3

Version 1.0

Cover design by Code Green Publishing

Published by
Code Green Publishing
Coventry, England

www.codegreenpublishing.com

For Horst, Linde, The Hard Tickets and all
our friends in Bavaria

Dinner Out first appeared in the 'Cork Literary Review'

The Pass first appeared in 'The Second Blackstaff Book of Short Stories'

Ted was broadcast on RTE Lyric FM

Arthur and Jess was broadcast on RTE Radio 1

Table of Contents

Ted

Brenda fixed a large sprig of holly behind 'The Return after Balaclava' in the hall. She stood down from the chair as the doctor came down the stairs and stood back to let him into the sitting-room and followed, closing over the door. It was getting dark and the lights on the tree looked pathetic in a room that hadn't been decorated for years. Now that Brenda was the only one of the family at home the room was used only at Christmas. She turned on the light and spoke first.

'She's failing.'

'I'm afraid she is,' the doctor replied.

'How long do you think?'

'It's hard to say, but I'd be surprised if it's more than a week or two, but you know what a strong-willed woman she is. If she decides to hold on it could be longer.'

Brenda shut the door.

'Do you think she knows?'

'She must know this will be her last Christmas. She said something about Ted coming.'

'That's my youngest brother. The last time we heard from him was a card from Sydney, Australia, eight years ago. We don't know if he's alive or dead, but she's never given up hope. Every Christmas she expects him to walk in and surprise us.'

'How long has be been in Australia?'

'We don't know if he is in Australia. About six months before the card arrived he had gone to England. After two weeks he phoned and we've heard nothing from him since apart from the card. We tried all the usual channels and Frank, my oldest brother, went to Sydney five or six years ago. For ten days he tried everything and could find no trace, but mother still thinks he'll come home.'

Brenda went ahead of the doctor into the hall and let him out. She took the scraps of holly from the hall-table to the kitchen and went upstairs to the bedroom.

'The doctor says that all things considered you're not so bad.'

Her mother whispered out loud, with a break for intake of breath:

'The cheek of him, what does he mean, "all things considered"?'

'Well you are eighty-six, and you have had two heart attacks.'

'Eighty-five, dear, and one heart attack.'

'Two, mother, I've told you before; the last turn you had was a heart attack.'

Immediately Brenda regretted her tone of voice; directness was a habit she had developed over the years to counter the 'forgetfulness' her mother used as a device to get her own way.

A gust of wind drove spatters of rain against the window. Brenda pulled the curtains and turned on the bedside lamp. It dimmed everything else in the room, leaving her mother and the upper half of her bed in a cosy pool of light. Since leaving work three years previously to look after her full-time Brenda oscillated between resentment at having to give up her job and a sense of satisfaction that she was doing her duty. Her resentment was not at having to look after her mother, but rather at the presumption of the others in the family that she was the one who would do it.

Brenda lifted her mother up and settled her pillows. Even that exhausted the old lady and she could feel her laboured breathing.

'Thank you, dear.'

She was unfailingly polite, which had always made it harder to resist her constant demands, but now she was not so demanding, using most of her energy to stay alive.

'I'm going to make you some scrambled egg.'

'Just a little, please.'

The old lady closed her eyes; Brenda was grateful she was not in pain. She straightened the sheet under her chin and went downstairs, hoping she would last until Christmas for the sake of the family. This year she wouldn't sit at the head of the table directing everything, as she had done for as long as Brenda could remember.

The scrambled egg and slice of toast looked sparse on the tray, and yet Brenda knew her mother wouldn't finish it; on principle she always left something. She put the tray on the bed-table, pulled it over and took the teapot onto the bedside cabinet.

'When will the doctor be here?' her mother asked.

'He's already been.'

'Oh.'

'He says you're doing fine but you must keep your strength up by eating.'

Over the days approaching Christmas physically her mother seemed to hold her own, but mentally she became more confused.

In the past it was always:

'Ted might surprise us this Christmas,' or 'If Ted comes this Christmas we'll have a party for him.'

None of them dared say more than:

'You'd never know,' or 'Good idea.'

His siblings didn't even talk among themselves about the possibility that Ted might have died, which was in fact less difficult for them to accept than that he was out there somewhere and wanted to cut off from them completely. When Frank had gone to Australia their hopes were tempered by the fear that he might trace Ted and find that he didn't want to know, or maybe discover he was in prison serving a long sentence.

The thing they agonised over most was what it was in Ted's childhood that might have made him a person who would want to disappear, but they couldn't come up with anything.

Ted had been the afterthought of the family and only four when his father died; not only did his mother spoil him but his brothers and sisters did too. He was bright but dropped out of school early against everybody's advice. After a couple of dead-end jobs he went to England. In the early years they all thought he would turn up but, as the years passed, hope faded. After Frank drew a blank in Australia, apart from his mother, they had only a dim hope that any of them would ever see him again.

The deteriorating condition of Brenda's mother dampened the run up to Christmas, and at one stage they thought of moving the day to Maura's house for the sake of the grandchildren, but decided against it. It would have upset the old lady and none of them would have relished having to explain to her that the excitement might not have been good for her. All their lives they had accommodated themselves to what she expected, as the easiest thing to do in the long run. If they did stand up to her or defy her she made life intolerable for days and sometimes even longer, by a combination of sarcasm, sulking and silence.

On the afternoon of the third day before Christmas Brenda brought her mother a piece of steamed plaice for lunch. As she put the tray on her bed-table her mother half sat up, turned her head slowly and looked her straight in the eye:

'When Ted arrives tell him to come up immediately, I want to talk to him.'

'Mother, Ted won't be coming home this Christmas.'

She squared her jaw.

'Yes he will, I know he will.'

'What makes you so sure?'

'He'll come because I'm not well.'

'I hope then you'll ask him where he's been,' Brenda said, not knowing how *compos mentis* her mother was, and playing along a little, feeling that feeding her fantasy could do no harm. There was a slight hesitation and then her mother said:

'Australia, of course.'

She lay back on the pillow.

'You can ask him too why he hasn't been in touch for so long?' Brenda said light-heartedly. She thought she might hear why her mother thought Ted had disappeared.

'You know why Ted went,' she said, 'but since none of you will tell me, I'll ask him. He'll tell me. Whatever it was that went on between you all, you'll have to be kind to him.'

This was the first intimation Brenda had that her mother believed something had gone on between Ted and the rest of the family that accounted for his not coming home.

Brenda opened her mother's napkin and tucked it into the neck of her nightdress. As she arranged her pillows and sat her up, her mother said matter-of-factly:

'What I really want to tell him is that I'm leaving him the house.' Brenda felt a weakness in her knees and sat down.

'What house?'

'This house of course, dear.'

Brenda allowed herself to feel what she had sublimated during the previous three years: real anger. It came in waves. She sat and watched her mother lying back on the pillows, chewing slowly. Brenda's mind became clouded; she was consumed with anger as her mother tried to put another piece of fish precariously onto her fork. Just before it reached her mouth it fell. She fumbled for it down her front and looked to Brenda for help. Brenda stood up, found it and left it on the side of her plate. Without a word, she secured a piece of fish on the fork and handed it to her mother. Her anger began to subside. She sat down and withdrew into a haze in her mind that partly obscured her mother from her. She could remember her in her prime, in total control managing and manipulating all of them. She had been a good mother, but on her terms. By the time Ted was born she had mellowed. Although she never lost the ability to get her own way, in recent years many of the habits of a lifetime had become empty and irritating rituals.

The old lady put down her fork, pushed her plate forward on the tray and lay back. Brenda folded her napkin and took away the bed-table.

'Will I plump your pillows?'

'No, thank you dear, they're fine.'

She closed her eyes, and Brenda took the tray and went downstairs. She washed the dishes and made tea. Taking a cup upstairs, she found her mother fast asleep and did not disturb her. In the evening Frank called on his way home from work. His mother said nothing to him about Ted and he didn't stay long.

During the week before Christmas Brenda's mother had rambled more often than she was coherent. She mentioned names of people who were long since dead; her husband and Stephen her favourite brother, but there was no further mention of Ted. On Christmas Eve the doctor came and found no deterioration in the old lady since his last visit. His prognosis was much the same: there would be no long term, but it was impossible to say how soon.

The family kept Christmas Day as normal as possible; Frank and his family came for lunch, and the others came during the afternoon. Each of the adults went up in turn to see their mother, but she didn't mention to any of them her expectation that Ted would come home for Christmas. They kept her informed about what was going on, but most of the time she dozed and wasn't with them. They observed all of the family rituals, but there was a cloud over everything. They left early except Maura who stayed to help with the clearing up and she volunteered to stay the night.

When the others had gone Brenda and Maura settled their mother and cleared the debris downstairs. They revived the fire and sat in the half-light of the Christmas tree lights. There was an exaggerated stillness after the activity of the day, and there was a quietness between them.

'I hear she was sure that Ted would come,' Maura said.

'Yes, and what's more she said the rest of us knew all along why he stayed away. So she believed all those years that there was a conspiracy between us.'

'And she never said a word.'

Maura and Brenda sat in silence gazing into the fire, and through it Brenda looked into the past and searched around for any situation in which her mother was not in control. She could find only one: Ted's disappearance. Even now the house revolved around her without her saying a word or knowing much about it for they had organised the day as she would have wanted. Totally dependent and not entirely with them, she was still in control, though it couldn't be for much longer. Brenda pictured her laid out in her bed upstairs and went over the funeral in her mind. Then despite having done it a thousand times before, she thought of all the reasons that Ted might have cut off from them all. She couldn't believe that if the worst had happened to him somebody would not have traced the family and let them know.

The shrill penetration of the doorbell shattered the silence and sent a shock wave through Brenda. Maura jumped. Neither of them spoke but looked at each other for a second. They both went out to the hall. Brenda hesitated and went towards the door.

'Ask who it is.'

She stopped. Through the door she said:

'Who is it?'

A man's voice whispered:

'It's me.'

They looked at each other. Neither of them recognised the voice.

'Who?' The voice came louder.

'It's me....Frank.'

Maura turned back down the hall while Brenda opened the door.

'Sorry, did I frighten you? Sally left her new teddy behind and she won't go to bed without it.'

They found the teddy and Frank went upstairs to see his mother. Brenda followed shortly in case the bell had wakened her. She met Frank coming out onto the landing. He put out his hands and took her hands in his.

'She's gone.' He drew Brenda to him and held her tightly for a moment before they went downstairs to tell Maura.

The following day, when making the arrangements they asked the undertaker to send a copy of the death notice to the Sydney newspapers.

The Hunt Ball

'I wish to God the Commander'd keep his fences,' said Spin as he tripped over barbed wire in the dark tearing his trousers and cutting his shin.

'Shut up and put that light out,' said Morty, 'or you'll have Kenny on our backs.' Morty and Spin spent much of their spare time trying to avoid Kenny the Commander's 'gamekeeper'. Kenny's father had been the gamekeeper in the old Colonel's time and he fancied the title and the work. In fact Kenny spent his time doing anything and everything around The Park, from chopping sticks to keeping an eye on the Commander's few surviving cattle. At night he made Morty and Spin's life difficult as they went about their business: snaring rabbits.

Kenny was not the only one living in the past. The Commander who was now elderly made few concessions to the passage of time; he was entirely unable to adapt. He was slightly fey, but a gentleman in every sense of the word.

The house was vast; twelve bedrooms, dining and drawing-room with a saloon between, a library, ballroom, billiard room, a host of other small rooms and a nursery wing. The Commander and his wife lived between the kitchen, the dining-room and the saloon. In cold weather they abandoned the saloon for a small room off the billiard room. The drawing-room was almost never used, there were rooms in the house that the family never entered from one end of the year to the other and the ballroom was used once a year for the hunt ball. In this mansion of a house one man was employed, Landers, to cook and to perform other essential household duties.

The people in the village treated the family indulgently. It was clear that in economic terms the village was in the ascendant and the family in decline.

'To hell with Kenny,' said Spin. 'I'm after cuttin' me leg.'

'Put the shaggin' light out, you can look at it later,' Morty shouted under his breath.

They picked their way through the wood to the fields beyond, to inspect the snares. When they had finished checking they had eleven rabbits; a good night's work. It was pitch black and the wood was uncannily still. Suddenly large drops of rain bombarded the trees and quickly penetrated to the two below. They quickened their pace along the track beside the high wall when suddenly a bright light ahead dazzled them. They were trapped. The wall was too high and the undergrowth on the other side of the track too dense.

'Mr Morton and Mr Moran,' came Kenny's voice sarcastically from behind a large flashlight.

Dropping the rabbits they turned and ran back to a spot where they could scale the wall and jump into the field on the other side. They crossed the ditch onto the road and, wet to the skin, walked back to the village.

This was it. Kenny had always threatened that when he caught them red-handed he'd have them up in court, and true to his word in due course Morty and Spin received summonses. They were fined five pounds each, but what galled them most was that Kenny had won and the court report in the local paper informed the whole countryside of their humiliation.

The event of the year at The Park was the hunt ball. It was the night the Commander and his wife came into their own, when the whole house came alive in a way reminiscent of the past. Weeks before the event, preparations began and Kenny, the outside man, and Landers, the inside man, who detested each other, did nothing else but prepare the house for the big event.

Landers was an ally of Morty and Spin, and Kenny was their common enemy. So when Morty decided that he and Spin were going to attend the hunt ball the first thing they did was to consult Landers. They confirmed that as it was a fundraiser for the hunt anyone could buy tickets; the only condition of admission was evening dress. They reckoned they could come up with the money if Landers could come up with the suits.

A week before the night, Morty received a message to say that he and Spin were to go to the kitchen door in the stable yard at ten o'clock the following evening. Landers met them and took them through the kitchen to a small room off the backstairs beside his bedroom. There he had two evening suits, one that had been the old Colonel's and the other a discarded one of the Commander's. Landers helped Morty with the Commander's suit and Spin with the Colonel's. The smell of mothballs nearly asphyxiated them, and with a supply of safety-pins Landers succeeded in getting the two into the suits. As soon as Morty was dressed he drew himself up to his full height and aping the Commander addressed Landers:

'Send me that fellow Kenny till I give him a piece of my mind,' and turning to Spin he declaimed: 'the man's a fool you know, a fool.'

'Take off the suits,' Landers said, 'I'll wrap them and bring them with you now.'

On the night of the ball Morty called to Spin's house for Spin's sister to help them into the suits. She had Spin togged out to look, more or less, like a gentleman in no time, and after much pulling and shoving Morty was as well presented as possible. Morty led the way down the village, his chest puffed out like a turkey cock, hoping as many people as possible would see him. Spin struggled to keep up hoping that nobody would notice him as he still wasn't convinced of the wisdom of the escapade.

Their entrance to the pub was greeted with a great cheer. Most of the regulars didn't think they would go through with it and in reparation for their doubting they kept buying them drink. Morty and Spin's resolution to get to The Park early went by the board as they revelled in the admiration of their drinking companions.

When 'time' was called the two were in good order. They headed up the village and, after a necessary stop behind one of The Park gates they made their way up the winding avenue, specially scuffled and edged for the occasion. When the house came into view it was ablaze with light and every window seemed to be open, letting out across the countryside the sound of the band and the boisterous noise of the dancers. Dusting down their suits and checking their ties they climbed the steps, presented their tickets at the door and went inside.

13

Morty and Spin knew the house well. They had worked in and around the place off and on, and had been through the house when the family was away, but this was the first time they had entered by the front door. Morty led the way through the inner hall to the passage leading to the ballroom from where the sound of music was deafening. They entered by the gallery and looked down on the mass of people on the floor below. It was packed. Despite open windows the heat was overpowering. The young couples, men in shirtsleeves and their partners mostly bare shouldered, were throwing themselves around with scant regard for anybody or anything, least of all the music, and crashing into older and more sedate couples trying, with great difficulty, to dance with some dignity. Morty and Spin retreated to the hall and went to look for the bar, which they found in the billiard room. The table was covered with boards on which the bottles were set out. The barmen were two men from the village.

'Begod Morty, I hardly knew you,' said one of them when they came to the head of the queue, and to Spin, 'Well aren't ye the gas men.'

'No doubt,' said Morty imperiously, ignoring the comment, 'you haven't draught?'

His suspicion confirmed, he ordered two bottles of stout. 'We need all the help we can get,' he added. They took their drinks and had no sooner settled into two chairs in the hall than there was a deafening blast on a hunting horn to announce that supper was served. They finished their drinks and followed the crowd towards the dining-room where supper was served buffet style. With substantial helpings the two made for the hall again and finding their seats occupied, sat on the floor and balancing their plates with great difficulty on their knees, began to eat.

'Ah, Morton and Moran,' came the Commander's voice from above them.

With the fright they began to struggle to their feet, in the course of which Spin upended his plate into Morty's lap. Morty began to brush himself down helped by the Commander.

'Thank you, sir, thank you sir,' said Morty, 'I'm fine,' not wanting him to pay too close attention to the suit.

'Good of you to support us. I hope you're enjoying the evening,'

'Yes sir,' they said in unison.

The commander moved on. He was in high spirits; it was his big night and it was going well; his only anxiety was the power supply. The house hadn't been re-wired since electricity was first installed and fuses blew easily with overloading. Every year for the hunt ball the Commander armed Kenny with a set of replacement fuses, and ordered him, on pain of his life, to stand by the fuseboard in the basement passage in case of emergencies.

The meal over, the music started up again. Morty and Spin went to the bar for more stout and took it back to the hall, which had been invaded by two groups of young bloods, who, cheered on by their ladies, faced each other across the hall. Uncorking bottles of champagne, they pointed them in menacing fashion at each other. There were two almost simultaneous pops and loud cheers as the two 'gunners' sprayed each other and everybody else in the hall.

'Gintlemen how are ye!' said Morty as the two escaped along the passage towards the ballroom.

'The time has come,' said Morty as Spin followed him along the passage and down the backstairs.

'Where are we going?' asked Spin.

'You don't think we came here to put up with that class of bad breedin'' replied Morty. 'Follow me and go aisy.'

Spin followed Morty down the stairs and along the basement passage. There was no one there, but they could hear voices from the kitchen. Morty sent Spin to make sure that the door to the stable yard at the end of the passage was open. It was.

'Stay where you are,' Morty ordered Spin, and he turned back towards the kitchen where the fuseboard was high up on the passage wall. A stepladder was in place with a box of fuses on top. He could hear Kenny's voice coming from the kitchen. Morty climbed the ladder gingerly and screwed out the main fuse. The house was plunged into darkness. The girls in the kitchen screamed. Morty put the fuse in with the spares and taking the box stole along the passage to Spin. Outside they stood at the door and listened. They heard Kenny swearing as he crashed into the steps. Recovering, he climbed the ladder to find the box gone. He swore again. Somebody produced a torch. They heard the Commander's voice:

'Kenny it's the main fuse, put in the spare.'

'Yes, sir,' said Kenny, 'but I can't find it, sir.'

'What do you mean?' barked the Commander. 'It's in the box with the others.'

'The box is gone,' replied Kenny.

'What do you mean it's gone? Gone where? Don't be stupid man, find it.'

'Come on,' Morty whispered to Spin, and the two made their way across the stable yard and out through the paddock. When they were two fields away Morty threw the box of fuses into the ditch and they stopped and looked back. They stood for a moment in the moonlight while Morty turned his back to the house and lit a cigarette. The house was silent and in total darkness. 'Good Old Kenny,' said Morty, in mock idiom of the big house.

They made their way across the fields towards the cover of the wood.

'Sure when we're this far,' said Spin, 'we might as well check the snares.'

The Archivist

Michael St John Mulhall was granny-reared. At least that was what he told his fellow seminarians to account for the absence of family of any kind. None of his colleagues liked to ask him exactly what this meant. They knew he was older than his classmates and they made the assumption that his granny was dead for they knew he was alone in the world. During holiday periods Michael stayed on in the seminary and took part in the life of the Community and he was happy to do so. He loved the round of the daily liturgy and outside term time he continued to study simply because he loved it.

Michael was short and inclined to weight but not yet stout; a condition he would not postpone much longer. He had a round smiling face and a winning manner. He hadn't a bad bone in his body nor had he an unkind thought in his head. He was gentle, kindly, thought the best of everybody and he was completely happy at what he was doing – preparing for the priesthood. He was excused work on the seminary's farm, in fact he was, by temperament, unfitted to survive in the real world.

Church history was his great passion, and especially the documentary sources upon which the history of the early Christian Church was based. He knew the scholarly works on the subject, but his great desire was to see some of the original documents. So much so that the Order arranged through a contact in Rome that during one long summer vacation Michael would work in the Vatican Archive.

He had never been out of the country before but he took it all in his stride. A priest of the Order met him at Rome airport and brought him to his quarters in their House, where he was as popular with his confreres as he had been back in Ireland. He soon found his way around and travelled every day on public transport to and from the Vatican. He worked from nine to five under a senior archivist who found him both congenial and willing to learn. Those above him noted his innate intelligence and the breadth of his knowledge for one, on the face of it, so inexperienced in the field.

The summer passed all too quickly for Michael and he was back in time for the new autumn term at the seminary. He had found his métier. He would be an archivist. It was already clear to the Order that he had a number of the gifts necessary to make a good one. He had a natural sense of history and its importance for understanding the present, an immense pleasure in handling and working with ancient documents and an instinct for their preservation. He had two further qualities that would stand him in good stead; patience, and contentment working on his own. A glowing account of Michael's summer in the Vatican Archive from his supervisor there to his Superior in Ireland confirmed what the Order already knew.

Michael did not have a particular friend amongst his year. He was equally friendly with, and liked by, all of them. On the day of their ordination any of them would have been happy to include him in their family occasion. John, the one who lived in the town where the cathedral was, invited him to join in his celebration. His family was delighted to host such a gentle, kindly, unobtrusive soul on such a special day in his life and all went well. Michael asked no questions and he told no lies. He was quite happy to account for himself to John's family in the way he accounted for himself to anybody when it was appropriate to do so, by telling them simply that he was granny-reared.

The Order signed Michael up for a two-year university archivist diploma which he began the autumn after his ordination. At the end of the two years he came first in his class and stayed on for another year to complete a degree. He was then set to a task that pleased him greatly: to establish an archive for the whole Province of his Order and to locate it in the House where he had been a seminarian.

Michael was in heaven. He was doing the work he loved. It involved occasional trips away, both around the country and to Rome, and he was in touch with the Order's mission stations abroad. He was also fully part of the life of the Community that he considered 'home.' After three years he had established the archive and collected together all significant documents from the Order's foundation to the present day. It had been hard work but satisfying and his enthusiasm attracted Father Keane, a retired member of the Community, who he trained as his assistant.

One morning after breakfast Michael's Superior, Father Ryan, sent for him. He was anxious when he received the message. His Superior, though tolerant of Michael's work since his Superior in Rome had ordered it, didn't lose an opportunity to make it plain that with the shortage of vocations, an archivist was a luxury the Order could not afford. Every man should be out in the field, and Michael dreaded the possibility that he might be sent to teach in a school or sent to a mission station abroad.

He knocked on Father Ryan's door.

'Come in. Ah Father Mulhall, sit down.'

The formal greeting served only to increase Michael's anxiety. He sat in front of the large mahogany desk covered with a litter of papers that emphasised to him how far apart he and his Superior were. He was nervous, as his original commission to establish the archive had been completed and he knew that the retired Father Keane was more than competent to maintain it on his own.

'I have received from Rome a note from the Superior General,' continued Father Ryan.

Michael's mind raced ahead. He was fearful that Rome was taking the same line as the man at the far side of the desk; that none of the Order's manpower was to be deployed on, what Father Ryan often referred to as, 'work inessential to the Mission of the Order as laid down by our Founder.' Father Ryan continued: 'The Superior General has received a letter from the Vatican with the instruction that you are to be posted to work in the Vatican Archive.'

Michael couldn't believe it. He had arrived in the Superior's study anxious and, though he had not yet said a word, he was now ecstatic.

'I think, Father Mulhall, you are probably aware that I personally do not approve of the deployment of our limited manpower on inessential work. But I am a man, as you are, under orders and we must obey. Your appointment takes immediate effect. The Bursar will make arrangements for your flight and you will stay at our House in Rome.'

'Thank you, Father,' was all that Michael said, fearful that anything else might sound triumphalist. He would honour his vow of obedience no matter what, but when the orders he received exceeded his wildest dreams, he had a strong sense that someone somewhere was looking after him – his granny.

Michael arrived at the Community House in Rome and started work at the Vatican Archive the following Monday. The archivist he worked under when he was a student, and whom he liked, was still there, but now Michael was fully qualified with three years' experience under his belt. In no time he was into a weekday routine between the city bustle, the musty quiescence of the archive and the security of the liturgical life of the House. At weekends he used his free time to explore the ancient and artistic treasures of Rome.

Slowly Michael was given responsibility in the Archive and soon he was working by himself on projects that required him to read more and more about the background of the documents with which he was dealing. He did this reading in his own time and derived great satisfaction from his expanding knowledge. He was totally absorbed in his work and as an archivist he had moved from his early experience of one small part of the Church, his own Order, to some of the seminal documents of the Church Universal.

Michael was not personally ambitious. He did not see himself as having a career in the Church, but a vocation of service. He did, however, allow himself to feel a little pleased when he was given limited access to the inner sanctum: the Vatican's Secret Archive. His conditions of access were spelled out carefully to him and any work he undertook there was under the careful supervision of his senior. One thing was borne in on him above all, he was not to browse; he was to go directly to the documents he needed for his work. He had no idea what the Secret Archive contained but assumed, whatever it was, it was material that didn't reflect well on the Church that claimed to be the continuing presence of Christ in the world. He saw no reason, however, why any archival material of the Church should be secret. If there were documents that showed up faults and failings the Church should admit them, apologise if necessary, and move on. Human failings, even of Popes of the past, were not the responsibility of succeeding generations of the Faithful.

One morning he found amongst a package of papers he was working on in the Secret Archive, a document that had no connection with other papers that were with it. Michael searched exhaustively and found that it was not catalogued anywhere. There was no record of its existence. When he translated it he found that it was a parchment that showed unequivocally that in the fourth century Apostolic Succession had been lost for over a hundred years. He knew that if this parchment were genuine it was, for the Church, an earth-shattering discovery. The Church's doctrinal authority depended on the continuity of Apostolic Succession; the unbroken succession of the consecration of bishops and so of Popes started by Christ's original commission to Peter. If it were proved that this succession was lost, as the document proved, and Apostolic Succession was not valid, the whole edifice of the Church's doctrine, its authority and even the Church itself would come crashing down.

Michael said nothing to anybody and replaced the document where he found it in order to allow him time to think. He knew that the key question now was whether it was genuine or a forgery. He also knew that over the centuries the Church had used many false documents to establish or buttress her authority; documents that were later proved to have been forged. He knew well of the best known cases, the False Decretals of Constantine and of St Isidore, and he wanted to establish for himself, before alarming others, whether this document was genuine or not.

When the time was opportune Michael took out the parchment again and by every means he knew of, including the preliminary scientific tests available to him, he concluded that it was genuine. He replaced it while he thought further about what to do. One option he considered, but for no more than a split second, was to destroy it secretly. To do so would run contrary not only to his nature, but to his deep instincts as an archivist. His only other option, since the matter was not his responsibility, was to show the document to his immediate superior. This he did but without declaring that he had made his own evaluation of it. When he arrived home that evening the Superior of the Order House was waiting for him.

'Michael, I have no idea what this is about, but I have an order from Cardinal Lucignano. Until further notice you are not to discuss any aspect of your work with anybody. You are not to receive or make phone calls, write or receive letters, you are to be accompanied to and from work and apart from that you are not to leave the House until further notice.'

Michael knew exactly what it was about, but kept his counsel.

The Superior himself accompanied Michael to work next morning. The chief archivist met him and called him into his office.

'Michael, it is clear that the document you found is a forgery, but it has been sent for scientific analysis. Even though it is a forgery I am to inform you that you are, under pain of excommunication, never to discuss it with anybody. It might become the source of unwarranted rumour or scandal. When it has been confirmed that it is a forgery, it will be placed in the Apostolic Penitentiary, which as you know is under the sole control of the Holy Father. Until then you are to be incommunicado, lest unwittingly you say something to somebody that might be taken up wrongly.'

Michael was aware of the catastrophic implications for the Church if the document were genuine, which he himself believed it was. Constant surveillance took its toll on him and he became depressed. Even at work when he went up the external metal stairs to the Loft, where he needed to go from time to time, his senior went with him.

One morning when he arrived into work Michael received word that he was to attend a meeting in the very heart of the Vatican itself. He turned up at the appointed time and knocked on the large elaborately sculptured wooden doors. When he entered there were three cardinals, none of whom he knew even by sight, sitting behind a long table covered with a green cloth.

'Father Mulhall, thank you for coming,' the cardinal in the middle said in a voice that seemed to Michael to stop just short of obsequious. 'Please sit down.'

Michael sat on the single chair on his side of the table. The middle cardinal continued:

'Father Mulhall, I know you realised immediately you found it that the document you discovered recently is a forgery. I can now confirm for you that after exhaustive analysis by the best international authorities, historical and scientific, this is in fact the case. As an experienced and highly thought of archivist you will know more about this process of analysis than we do.' All three cardinals smiled artificial smiles; the first time the other two showed the slightest sign of animation. 'As you are also aware, throughout history there have always been people who wanted to harm the Church, and things are no different today. If word of this document reached the ears of certain people they would choose to claim that it was authentic in order to make trouble for the Church. Can you imagine what a hostile press could make of it? We in the Church have more to do with our time than waste it countering spurious claims, therefore those few of us who are aware of this document's existence have been put under a permanent interdict by the Pope never to speak of it again.'

There was a long pause and then the cardinal asked, 'Father Mulhall, is there anything you would like to say?' After another pause, Michael began:

'Your eminence, I want to assure you that since I was ordained I have never, even in the smallest thing, dishonoured my vow of obedience. However, I would impugn my personal integrity if I did not tell you that, having considered the matter carefully, I believe that the document I discovered in the Archive is genuine.'

There was a long silence during which none of the three looked at Michael. His two colleagues sitting impassively at either side of him looking down at the table, the cardinal spokesman responded:

'We are of course confident, Father Mulhall, that you will never dishonour your vow of obedience, especially concerning an order from the Holy Father himself. It is clear, however, from the opinion of others and from the experts we consulted that your opinion of the document is mistaken. Thank you for coming and good morning.'

Michael stood up, bowed slightly, turned and left the room. On his way back to the Archive he reflected that he had no idea where the courage to give his own professional opinion had come from, but he was glad that he did.

The routine, established since Michael found the document, which he now wished he had never discovered, continued as before. Despite the interview, or maybe because of it, he was still under surveillance.

Later that week Michael needed to go to the Loft to consult a particular document stored there. As had now become the norm, his senior went with him. When he found what he was looking for and had made his notes he went out onto the landing of the steps. His senior followed him and locked the door. The next thing

Michael was falling down the metal stairs and tumbled the whole way to the bottom where he landed in heap on the ground. His senior hurried quickly down. There was no movement from Michael. He checked one wrist and then the other. There was no pulse. He opened his shirt. He watched carefully for a minute. There was no movement of his chest. Father Michael St John Mulhall had gone to be with his granny. His Order mourned a much loved member and the Church was deprived of a first-class archivist.

Dinner Out

'Hurry Mum, they're going without me.' Kate's third and youngest cried as she struggled to tie his shoelace. When she finished he ran for the door, his schoolbag jumping up and down on his back.

'Stay away from the puddles in the lane,' she shouted after him as he ran to catch up with his brother and sister on their way to the road to wait for the school bus. Paddy, her husband, had left around six to queue for the mart and unless he had a miraculous change of habit he wouldn't be home until the small hours of the morning, much the worse for wear. She endured patiently his obsessive hard work and his drinking and looked forward to the peace and quiet of a day like this when he was away all day.

Kate turned on the radio and cleared the table. She always listened to the morning magazine programmes; they kept her in touch with the outside world, which she missed since she became a farmer's wife. She had been born and brought up in the town and lived there until she married, and although she loved the country there were times she found it lonely. She had just started washing-up when the phone rang. She dried her hands and went into the hall.

'Hello.'

'Is that Kate?'

'Yes'

'This is George.' She scrambled around in her head and drew a blank.

'George who?'

'Has my voice changed that much?'

'George,' she said, tumbling to it. 'Where are you?'

'In town. How are you?'

'I'm fine. What are you doing in town?'

'I'm staying overnight; I'm on my way to the boat in the morning. How's Paddy?'

'He's fine.'

'Could you both have dinner with me to-night? I'm staying at Lawlor's.'

'Paddy isn't here. He won't be back until late.'

'Well can you come?'

'I just might be able to contact Paddy at the mart.'

'Fine, but if you can't contact him, come yourself.'

'Are you sure you're not just being polite?'

'Of course not, I'd love to see you.'

'What time and where?' Kate asked.

'Lawlor's at eight.'

'Thank you, George. I'll try and contact Paddy right away.'

'See you later,' he said and hung up.

Kate stayed sitting at the telephone giving free rein to her memory. She had gone out with George for almost two years. It was through him she met Paddy; they were friends at the rugby club. It was quite a while before Paddy asked her out, which in no way affected Paddy and George's friendship. When they came to be married she knew Paddy would have asked him to be his best man but he had gone to Canada and after Christmas cards for a couple of years they lost touch.

George was tall and well-built with a fair complexion and sandy hair. He was a natural gentleman who would hold the door open not only for a woman but for a man too, for no other reason than it wasn't in him to go first. His good manners were no mere formality; he was sensitive to others and genuinely self-effacing in the nicest possible way. Everybody liked George, and most of the girls were crazy about him but, apart from Kate, he treated them all the same.

She picked up the phone and dialled the mart.

'Could you get Paddy Martin for me please?'

'Hold on.'

She could hear the public address: 'Telephone call for Paddy Martin, will Paddy Martin please come to the phone.'

She waited. After a while a voice said: 'Did he not come?'

'No.'

'Hold on a minute I'll try outside.' In a while he came back.

'He was here earlier, but he's gone.'

'If he comes back will you ask him to ring home please?'

'OK.'

'Surely he doesn't start as early as this,' Kate thought. 'I'll try one of the pubs later.' She knew most of his haunts, but it wasn't easy to get him as he tipped off the barmen to say he wasn't there. She didn't hold out much hope of contacting him unless she toured the pubs herself, and she was determined not to suffer that humiliation again.

Kate went back to the kitchen to finish the washing-up. The radio fought a loosing battle with her memories of the carefree days of fifteen years ago and more. She remembered them as good times, not just George, but her girlfriends and the whole gang. One by one they were married. She reflected that it is a choice between the net happiness of bachelorhood or the net happiness of marriage. The trouble is that bachelorhood is tagged failure and marriage success, and fourteen years into marriage Kate knew that this was an over-simplification and even a distortion of the truth. It suddenly occurred to her that she didn't know if George had married. She assumed he hadn't or he'd have said something, but it might be that he is just travelling alone.

Kate finished the washing-up, her mind still buzzing. She went upstairs to make the beds. When she had made her own bed she went to the wardrobe and took out some outfits and held dresses up to herself looking in the mirror matching this with that and indulging her passion for good clothes. She and Paddy went out a couple of times a year to the IFA and Hereford Breeders' dinner dances for which she always had something new; Paddy for all his faults wasn't mean, but he never noticed what she wore. Kate surprised herself and became excited at the prospect of having dinner alone with George, and she felt free to do so since she had made a genuine effort to contact Paddy. She was now beginning to hope that he wouldn't get the message at the mart. George had been careful to say to come herself if she couldn't contact him.

Then she lapsed into an intimate fantasy with George and brought herself back to reality by thinking it likely he would have a wife with him. She put away all of her clothes without deciding finally what to wear.

Kate went downstairs and collected her thoughts to plan everything in readiness for her evening out. She started to get dinner ready for the children; Paddy always had his meal out on mart day.

'Fourteen years is a long time, George might be fat and bald,' she thought. 'I've certainly put on weight and I'm sure he has too.' She started to feel anxious that after the preliminaries they might run out of things to say and began to half hope that Paddy would get her message. She had the children's dinner ready to put on and went out to the yard to feed the pet lambs that were her pin-money. She imagined the kind of life she would have had if she had married George: a fine semi, or even detached house in Toronto or wherever he lived, and all that went with a comfortable middle-class suburban existence. No muck and dirt and worries about the weather and the price of cattle, and above all no husband coming in drunk at night.

She had just finished the lambs when the telephone bell in the yard shattered her fantasy, and on her way inside she couldn't decide whether she wanted it to be Paddy or not. She lifted the phone.

'Is Paddy there?' She took the message and realised she was glad.

Kate put on the dinner for the children and made herself a snack lunch. She began to waver again between looking forward to tonight on her own and half hoping that Paddy would be there. He usually had his lunch at the mart, so she phoned again.

She wanted to be able to tell him and George, if she couldn't contact him, that she had tried twice and left a message both times. No, he hadn't been back and they would definitely give him the message if he turned up. She was sure now that it was going to be a normal mart day and Paddy wouldn't be home until the small hours.

The children arrived in from school and had their dinner. Kate sent the middle one, Pat, to the cottage at the end of the lane to ask Mary if she could baby-sit. She felt unsettled and decided the only way to put in the time was to do some hoovering. She took out the hoover and did most of the house, then she left the children's tea ready and went upstairs to wash her hair. She spent time doing her nails and went through her clothes again trying things on and finally selecting what she would wear. She went downstairs, made the children's tea and called them. When Julie, the eldest, saw the curlers she asked:

'Where are you going, Mum?'

'I'm going to meet an old friend of your Dad's and mine.'

'What's her name?'

'It's not a her it's a him, his name is George.'

'Is Dad going too?'

'I don't think so, George phoned after breakfast and I can't contact Dad. It's mart day and he'll be away all day.'

'Where does George live?'

'Canada.'

'And where are you meeting him?'

'He's invited us for dinner in Lawlor's.'

'Mum, you can't go out for dinner with a man; if Dad's not there, everyone'll think you're having an affair.' And they all laughed, including Kate.

'Of course they won't. He's just an old friend, and really he was Dad's friend.'

'But if anyone sees you they won't know that.'

'They can think what they like,' replied Kate and thought how ridiculous it was that a man and woman can't be seen together without people's tongues wagging, yet she knew that was the way it was, and resented her thirteen year old daughter reminding her.

Kate cleared the table as the children became absorbed in their favourite 'soap'. She washed up and went upstairs to get ready. She was in good time and soaked in the bath, going over in her mind what she remembered of her courtship with George. All her memories were good and stirred inside her a warm feeling the like of which she had long since forgotten. For a few precious minutes she felt free of all the responsibilities the last fourteen years had brought. She was entirely on her own indulging her body and her mind as though husband and family and everything else didn't exist. The water started to go cold so she draped a towel around herself and went to the bedroom. She began to dress, selecting each item carefully, and when she finished she did a couple of turns in front of the mirror and allowed that she was pleased. She sat down on the stool in front of the dressing table to try on jewellery. Julie pushed the door open and came in.

'That's nice Mum, but I don't like the earrings.' Kate tried another pair.

'Is that better?' Kate asked, fastening the hasp of the necklace that went with them. Julie agreed it was and picked out a brooch that she held to her mother's dress and which they both agreed was just right. Kate put on some perfume.

'That's your special perfume, Mum, isn't it?' Julie said with a conspiratorial grin.

'Yes love, it is, but I don't often get a chance to use it, you see the lambs don't like it.'

'I hope George does,' Julie said laughing as she danced to the door pulling it behind her.

When Kate arrived downstairs Mary was there. Kate enquired about homework, gave the usual instructions about bedtime, which she knew would be ignored, and left. As she crossed the yard to the shed her heart sank; Paddy had taken the car and left the Land Cruiser.

'Not the end of the world,' she thought, 'but a bit of a letdown.'

Kate arrived at the hotel and immediately recognised George waiting at the door. He didn't see her getting out of the jeep and she had time to see that he was heavier, with hair thinner and receding. As she went up the steps he saw her. He smiled broadly and came down towards her.

'Kate,' he said, and kissed her on both cheeks. Holding her firmly by the upper arms he stood back and looked her straight in the eye.

'You haven't changed a bit.'

'Oh George, there's much more of me than there used to be.' He stood back and looked her up and down.

'A little, perhaps, but nothing stays the same.' Holding her under one arm he walked her up the steps and held the door open for her.

In the foyer he asked: 'Would you like a drink here or will we go into the bar?'

'Here's fine,' she replied, and he went and ordered their drinks. When he returned he sat beside her on the sofa, turning sideways to look straight at her.

'I couldn't contact Paddy. I tried the mart twice and left a message. He'll be sorry to miss you. What time do you leave in the morning?'

'The ferry leaves at seven.'

'Unless he drops in here by chance I'm afraid you won't see him, and this isn't one of his haunts.'

'Be sure to give him my best regards and tell him how sorry I was to miss him. What family have you?' he asked.

'Three, a girl and two boys. Are you married yourself?' she asked.

'I was but we divorced three years ago.'

'Have you children?'

'No, but tell me about you.'

'There's nothing much to tell really,' she said and told him a bit about the farm and the children. He was genuinely interested and Kate was reminded how when you were talking to George he made you feel like the only person in the world that mattered. She relaxed quickly and their conversation flowed. They finished their drinks and had another. George asked for the menu and handed it to Kate. The waiter went away and when he came back they were still talking. They stopped talking, gave their order and took up again where they had left off. Kate had a warm feeling deep inside and found herself fantasising that it was she and George. The waiter came to call them. As Kate walked across the dining-room she felt ten feet tall and didn't care who saw her, she was feeling like a woman for the first time for years. She knew exactly why people had affairs and didn't blame them. She remembered what Julie had said and how they had all laughed.

The light in the dining-room was dim and they were at a table for two at the end of the room. As they faced each other across the table, for Kate everybody else in the world except George evaporated and there was scarcely a break in the conversation. She abandoned herself to this time out of life and savoured every minute. She even resented the intrusion of the waiter. It was years since she felt so relaxed and light-hearted. She had planned to tell George where all the rest of their gang were and what had happened to them, but he didn't enquire and she decided not to. She enjoyed her meal without taking much notice of it, despite George's repeated concern that it was all right.

When the coffee came Kate looked at her watch. It was twenty past eleven. She didn't want the night to end but knew she would have to leave soon to let Mary home. They finished and went back to the foyer.

'I'm afraid I must go. That was a really lovely evening George, thank you.'

'Must you, so soon?'

'I'm afraid so. I have to let the baby-sitter home; she has to be up for school in the morning.'

'I hope you have enjoyed to-night as much as I have,' he said.

'I've enjoyed it more than I can say.'

'If there is any chance that you and Paddy can come to Canada I would be delighted to put you up.'

'I don't think there's much chance, but thank you.'

George held the door for Kate and took her arm going down the steps.

'Give my best to Paddy and tell him how sorry I was not to see him.' George continued to hold Kate's arm as they crossed the carpark. At the Land Cruiser Kate took out her keys and opened the door. She turned around and said: 'thank you again George that was a lovely evening.'

'It was a great pleasure for me,' he replied and holding her firmly he kissed her gently on the lips and then held the door while she sat in. He stood back as she started the engine and waved as she drove out of the carpark.

Kate drove home slowly, her head buzzing. When she arrived Mary was asleep at the cooker. After she left, Kate checked the children. She went to her room, kicked off her shoes and lay on the bed remembering every detail of her time with George.

She undressed and went to sleep.

She woke, as usual, to the bang of the car door in the yard. On nights like this Paddy came to bed in three instalments: the noise in the yard, the clattering in the kitchen while he looked for something to eat and his eventual arrival upstairs. Kate pretended to be asleep when he arrived into the bedroom. She hated the stench of alcohol more than the noise. In bed, as usual, he was asleep before her.

The Visitor

Mikey sat on the windowsill of his cottage enjoying the warmth of the late afternoon summer sun. He kept an eye for the odd passer-by with whom to pass the time of day. He had lived in the village all his life and recently found for the first time that he didn't know some of the younger people; children and grandchildren of people he had grown up with. A large silver-coloured car pulled up on the far side of the street driven by a well-dressed man wearing a brightly coloured shirt and a cravat. Mikey glanced at him but took no notice until the man crossed to his gate. Nobody from a car like that ever came to Mikey's door before. He looked again.

'Well Holy God and His Blessed Mother is it yourself.'

'It is.'

Bob shook Mikey's arthritic hand, a little too strongly. Mikey lifted his behind off the windowsill.

'Well it's a quare few years since I saw you.'

'It is, it's thirty-five at least. How did you know me?'

'Sure I'd know you anywhere from your mother. You're the spittin' image of her and don't I remember you in short pants goin' around the place bouncin' a ball, a little black ball, and you'd be throwin' it out with a spin on it and have it comin' back to you. I do often think o' that.'

'And, Mikey, how are you keeping?'

'I can walk and I can talk, and when you're well over eighty and you can do that you're not so bad, and your poor mother and father long since dead and gone, Lord have mercy on them. They were lovely people. They were back here about eight or ten years ago. That was the last I saw of them and I heard that they both died up in a slap one after the other shortly afterwards. And where's your sister, and I have to tell you I've forgotten her name?'

'June is in Canada.'

'Come in and sit down.'

Mikey took his stick and limped through the open door of his cottage into the dark kitchen.

'Me Missus died six years ago and I'm on me own ever since.'

'That's lonely for you.'

'It is, but you have to get used to it. The night-time is the worst. The 'Meals on Wheels' do bring me dinner and after that the cup o' tea and the odd boilt egg that I can manage meself. Put down that cat and sit there, you'll have to excuse the place, it's gone to the divil since she died. Angela, me daughter, comes in now and again and cleans the place up. I'm not able. I'm on this stick fifteen years or more. I went to Dublin and had one hip done about ten years ago, but never again. The nurses and doctors were great, but the pain; Holy God the pain was terrible. I'll put up with the other one, bad and all as it is. I don't be goin' anywhere anyway. Can't I see the whole world on television, and it's nothin' but bad news so I don't watch it. I look at the hurlin' and the football and that's the height of it. And where are you livin' now?'

'I live in Botswana.'

'Botswana, and where in the name of God is that?'

'It's in Africa.'

'I remember now; your mother and father told me you were in Africa. And how do you get on with all those black fellas? But they tell me you can't say that these days. I don't know what you're supposed to call them, but sure aren't they black, and what's the harm in that. I'm sure they call us white fellas. And what are you doin' there?'

'I'm an engineer.'

'And what possessed you to go to Africa?'

'After I qualified I was in a boring job in Dublin and I saw an ad in the paper. They were looking for engineers in Botswana so I applied and I've been there ever since.'

'I suppose you had a look at your father's old shop in the town. It's a supermarket this fifteen or twenty year. You serve yourself and you sink or swim. A neighbour brings me in once a week and I know where to find the few things I need. You don't get the service these days the way you did in your shop, and when you go to pay the young ones is talking to each other and you're only a nuisance to them. I bagged sugar and delivered groceries and did everything around the shop for your father, God be good to him. There wasn't much money in those days and he used give the poor people a bit off and let them pay at the end of the week, and if there was a death in a family he'd send up a few things to give them a bit of a help. He was a gentleman.'

Mikey opened a cupboard and took out a bottle of whiskey and poured two glasses.

'And what kind of work do you do in Africa?'

'I'm retired now, but I used to build roads and bridges.'

'And I suppose you don't live in a mud hut,' said Mikey, curious to know how Bob lived but not wanting to be too inquisitive.

'I live just outside the city in a house with a few acres of land; my wife used to keep horses.'

'I back the odd horse meself. Paddy, me neighbour, works in the town and lays the bets. It gives me a great interest in the evening paper that he drops in at night. I have the cottage acre out the back. It's enough to grow a few spuds, but I'm not able to do that now, and if you look out you'll see it's gone wild. A fella up the road used to cut the hay off it for his donkey, but everyone is so well off these days nobody wants it.'

'That's one thing about where I live, labour is cheap and the Africans are glad of the work inside and outside the house.'

'People can't get anyone to do anything round here they're all gettin' big money in the factories and the towns.'

'Does your Missus race the horses?'

'She used to race them. It was a great interest for her.' Bob looked around the kitchen. It was even smaller than the quarters for his servants at the end of his garden, if somewhat more comfortable.

'You'll see great changes around here. I suppose you had a good look around the town?'

'I did and I nearly didn't know it. There's not one shop front the same as when I was a child'

'When you were a child and I was working for your father, people were contented. Everyone has too much money these days and the young people's gone to hell with drink and drugs and the divil knows what. You said your wife used to keep horses. Did she give them up?'

'She still has horses, but we separated some years ago and she lives a couple of hundred miles away now with another man.'

'We have that class o' thing here too. Do you mind if I ask you, have you family?'

'I have two sons.'

'And do they live with you?'

'No, one's in Australia and the other's in South Africa.'

'So you're on your own?'

'I am, and answerable to no one.'

Mikey passed the bottle to Bob who poured himself more whiskey.

'That must be lonely. The furthest any of mine is is the city and they all drop in to keep an eye on the auld fella. Are your two married?'

Bob, mellowing from the whiskey, comfortable in the kitchen and at ease with the congenial Mikey was ready to tell the truth.

'Well Mikey the truth of the matter is I don't know. You see they left home one after the other in their early twenties when things were bad between my wife and myself and they haven't been in touch with me for years. All I know is that the older one is in Australia and what he's doing I have no idea and I'm sad to say the younger one is in prison in South Africa. As far as I know he was on drugs and then started to supply them. I think their mother is in touch with them from time to time but she's never in touch with me so I've no information.'

'Well isn't that shockin', and how do you account for that?'

'Their mother turned them against me early on and when they left home they never made contact again.'

Mikey began to wonder how in the name of God things could get so bad that two young men would want to have no contact with their father.

'And what do you do with your time now that you're retired?'

'I play a lot of golf and I travel.'

'Everyone's playin' golf in this country. Every second week there's a new golf course opening somewhere and as far as travel is concerned I believe that in the summer Dublin airport is like Croke Park on the day of an All Ireland. Everyone has the money and they can do what they like.'

'And what do your young people do?'

Angela lives in the town, Mary is married to a farmer in Wicklow and the three boys are in Dublin; one's an accountant, one's a teacher and the other is in the motor business. All married, and I have six grandchildren, and some of them call to see me from time to time.'

Mikey topped up Bob's drink.

'Your children all did well.'

'I suppose they did right enough. They all worked hard at school and the ones that studied afterwards used to work at jobs to keep themselves. They had to travel to the city to get work, a bit like yourself but not as far.'

The conversation flowed as long as they were talking about the past and about family, but when they had exhausted those interests conversation ran thin. The silences became longer and to fill some of them Mikey would top up Bob's glass and put no more than a dash into his own, or skip it altogether, until the bottle was finished.

This was the first time since he arrived in Ireland that Bob had been in a home. Hotels and restaurants, no matter how good don't give what Mikey supplied by his hospitality and his homely kitchen. Bob was conscious that he had started to slur his words and inevitably he fell asleep.

Mikey was relieved as he had run out of things to say. He put on the kettle to make tea and looked in the cupboard to see if he had enough to offer Bob something to eat when he woke up. He tidied a few things around the kitchen and in a while Paddy dropped in the evening paper. Mikey accounted for his sleeping visitor and Paddy remembered him. Mikey checked the nags, no luck, and when he had read the rest of the paper Bob was still asleep. Mikey put two eggcups, two plates and cutlery on the table.

When Bob had been asleep for more than an hour Mikey thought he ought to waken him; tea and some food wouldn't be out of place.

'I think it's time we had something to eat,' he said across the kitchen. His slumbering guest didn't move. Mikey said it again, this time louder. No stir. He went over, put his hand on Bob's shoulder and spoke again. The heavy breathing, just short of a snore, continued. Mikey shook him and patted him on the cheek but could not waken him. He shook him vigorously without success. He took his stick, went to the gate and asked a passer-by to call to Paddy and ask him to come.

Paddy arrived and couldn't rouse Bob either.

'If he wasn't breathin' so even and he didn't look so peaceful you'd be worried,' said Mikey, 'he musn't be used to the drop of whiskey.'

Paddy went back and brought Bridie. They half lifted and half dragged Bob down to the room and put him on Mikey's bed. He stirred, but didn't waken.

'It's nothin' new for me to sleep beside the cooker,' said Mikey, 'sure he'll be grand in the mornin'.'

.

The Tea Party

'Go and have a look at her, she should have calved long ago.'

'Yes boss.'

Dinny whistled over his shoulder for Bess and made for the avenue towards the pond field. It was one of the hottest days in a long hot summer; the pond had dried up. He had learned to move at a slower pace in the heat and even Bess when she arrived crossed over and back behind him only once before walking to heel. Dinny had spent all his working life with milking herds and even Fred would admit there wasn't much he didn't know about cows.

They passed the end of the house and along the side of the terraced lawn in front. The weeds that pushed above the scorched grass had been mown before lunch and Viv had set up a table with a white linen cloth in the shade of the two big beech trees. An assortment of chairs, parasols and other accoutrements of tea on the lawn had been left out and Viv was arranging cups, plates and cutlery on the table. She looked up as Dinny dispersed his escort of midges with his cap.

'They're bad to-day,' said Viv.

'They'd drive you mad, Ma'm.'

Dinny maintained his slow pace and continued down the avenue. Viv took her tray and crossed the lawn back to the house. She was one of those farmers' wives that played no part in the farm, and now that the girls had gone, she spent most of her time between the house, one or two organisations in the village and some social coming and going with a few friends. Fred was one of the best farmers in the area, and had little time for socialising, but was happy so long as Viv kept herself busy one way or another.

She climbed the steps to the terrace and went into the cool hall. The house was two floors and an attic above a damp basement where years ago servants used to work, and was now abandoned to rats and the storage of fuel. The attic, roasting in summer and freezing in winter, where the servants used to sleep, was now full of trunks, chests and other discarded items of another time. This collection was added to significantly after Fred's mother died when Viv made changes to make the house her own. She brought it up to date sensitively without in any way interfering with its essential character.

She had almost forgotten the early years of their marriage when her mother-in-law directed the domestic economy of the home. The old lady sat in her chair in the corner of the morning room and handed out the week's budget for the shopping. She kept the key of the linen cupboard and gave it to Viv only when needed, and to be returned immediately. In those days Fred coped with his divided loyalty to his mother and wife by having as little as possible to do with any matter that was of concern to both of them.

After she died, for a couple of years Viv stopped inviting any of her mother-in-law's friends, but when she became used to being mistress in her own home she established the practice of asking them to tea once during the summer. This she did because she felt sorry for the old ladies, most of whom were invalid, slightly deaf, lonely, or any combination of the three. She also felt a loyalty to Fred, despite the fact he did not inherit any of the social pretensions of his mother, not to sever connections with the families amongst whom he had grown up.

To-day was the day of the annual tea party. Viv did everything according to her mother-in-law's standard, so as not to give the old ladies anything to say, but despite making the effort she knew that some of them would dine out on her deficiencies for the rest of the year. Not all of them were what Viv described as 'foolish old women'. One or two were quite good company and anyway she treated the whole thing light-heartedly. She invited one of her own friends for support, a friend who was patient and kind to the old ladies but didn't take the whole thing too seriously.

Dinny arrived at the pond field and Bess went ahead while he opened the gate and closed it behind them. She heeled again as they crossed the field towards the herd. More than half of them were lying down, enduring the torment of the flies that crawled all over them. The occasional flick of an ear or swish of a tail was an effort. Those lying close to Dinny and Bess's path rose indolently and took a few steps away, turning and watching the progress of the man and the dog across the field. Dinny had marked out the cow in question and went towards her. She was lying down ahead, and as they approached she heaved as if to rise, bringing her front legs up but unable to budge her hindquarters. Dinny and Bess stopped. She tried again and seemed to be in two parts; the front active and the rere still. Dinny ordered Bess to stay and took a couple of paces forward. The cow kept her eye fixed on Bess but did not move. He walked around behind her and she made another effort to rise but barely moved her front legs as though she knew there was no point. Dinny put her tail aside to check her pins but couldn't see one of them properly the way she was lying. One way or another there was nothing to do but to bring her in.

Dinny and Bess made back across the field and up the avenue, which was blocked by a car left while a driver escorted two old ladies, one on a walking frame and the other on a stick, across the lawn. Viv came to meet them taking the arm of the one with the stick freeing the driver to return and move the car. The crippled convoy moved slowly across the lawn towards the table by the beech trees where Viv seated them in the shade.

'My dear, you're so kind to have us,' said Mary's oldest friend. Viv called her 'The Gunner,' because of the direct things she said and the way she shot questions at people. In the days when she could still garden she wore a tattered RAF World War II flying jacket. 'Mary would be so proud of you.'

Viv smiled across at her friend Ros and replied:

'I almost decided to postpone our party until the weather was cooler, but thought that outside and in the shade would be all right.'

'And who are you?' The Gunner shot at Ros.

Taken aback Ros gave her name.

'Oh, Barbara's daughter. I didn't recognise you.'

'No, her daughter-in-law.'

'Oh! Your mother-in-law was an old friend; we first met in Iraq during the war and ended up living only a few miles apart.'

'London.' Viv shouted into the wrong ear of Miss Butler, the other old dear.

'She's a journalist.'

'A Jesuit?'

'No, a journalist.'

'Oh, one of those; they're so rude, pushing those things into people's faces and asking impertinent questions. I'm sure she doesn't do that.'

'No, she writes for a newspaper.'

'Barbara didn't like Iraq,' said The Gunner detaining Ros, 'Desmond was an engineer and away most of the time. That's how we met. In fact we came home together and left the men there. How is Barbara's daughter, I've forgotten her name?"

'Patricia.'

'Didn't her marriage break up?'

'She's in Scotland. She and her husband live apart.'

'I never liked him, his eyes were too close together.'

Ros suppressed a smile and caught Viv's eye, as she adjusted a straw sun-hat with dangling anti-fly corks on Miss Butler, who hadn't heard.

'I haven't seen a hat like that for years. Not since Africa.'

Viv suppressed a smile. 'I'm sure that's where it's from; it's been in the attic since I came.'

Another car drove up the avenue and went straight into the yard; the other two guests had arrived together. They were fit enough to walk unaided. Viv went across the lawn to meet them.

The Gunner peered towards the two.

'Who have we now?'

'Miss Beatty and someone I don't know,' said Ros.

The old lady blinked and kept looking.

'It's Marjorie. Oh my God,' said The Gunner, 'we'll have nothing but cats. I hope you know something about cats or we won't get a word in edgeways.'

Ros confessed she didn't and Miss Butler, who hadn't heard, looked round.

'It's Harriet and Marjorie.'

Viv and the two latecomers arrived at the table. Ros stood up. Viv introduced Ros to Marjorie, who was the youngest of the four, and probably in her late seventies. Miss Beatty, already wearing a sunhat sat down and fanned herself with her hand. Viv left and went for the teapot.

'I can't get used to this heat,' said Miss Beatty.

'Don't fight it,' fired The Gunner, 'forget it; the more you talk about it the hotter you become.'

Miss Beatty kept fanning while she digested this piece of colonial wisdom. She turned to Miss Butler on her left and raised her voice.

'We're not to talk about the heat.'

'The heat.'

'Yes, it is hot, even in the shade,' said Miss Butler, 'I simply can't get used to it.'

'Well Marjorie how are the cats?' asked The Gunner, on the principle that attack was the best form of defence.

At this point Ros, feeling redundant, left the four and followed Viv to the house.

Dinny back in the yard with Fred:

'She can't move her hindquarters, we'll have to bring her in.'

'It's hardly milk fever before she's calved.'

'I don't think so boss, but I think she's close so we'll have to bring her in one way or the other.'

Dinny fixed up the tractor, and with Fred and Bess perched behind him drove down the avenue. Fred waved across to the old ladies from out the back of the cab and one of them waved back. Fred dreaded the thought of having to go and talk to them before they left. When his mother was alive he would have had to wash and change, but not now. If they didn't like him the way he was, that was their problem, but he knew that changing had been for his mother's sake rather than for her friends.

When they arrived at the field the cow again made an attempt to get up and failed. Dinny rocked her gently with his foot.

'I'd swear it's that leg.'

Fred walked around her and she made another attempt to rise.

'We'll get her up.'

Dinny lowered the buckrake with the board on it and backed up to the cow, gently easing the board under her. She rose her front quarters again and fell back. Dinny jumped down from the tractor and he and Fred heaved her bit by bit onto the board. They tied her on to stop her lunging, raised the buckrake and Dinny drove slowly with Fred and Bess walking behind. On the avenue the whole tea party turned to watch the progress of the 'ambulance.' In the yard

Dinny spread a thick bed of straw in the lean-to while Fred phoned the vet.

Viv and Ros arrived back to the old ladies with tea on two trays. The four were talking away in twos.

'………sold his place in Meath and is back in Curradoon. It was all getting too much at his age. He'll keep the mare and the hunter, not that he'll ever hunt again.'

'What a pity George wasn't interested.'

'He held on in the hope that he'd change his mind.'

Viv poured and Ros passed around.

'We're talking about Arthur,' said Marjorie to Miss Butler.

'Who?'

'Arthur Manders.'

'Poor man, does he go far?'

'No. Manders, he's coming back to Curradoon.'

'Oh, Arthur. Poor George; Arthur's trouble is he's good with horses and bad with people.'

Viv and Ros finished passing round and sat down. Viv had just poured for them when Miss Beatty upended her tea into her lap. Ros helped her up while she held her skirt away from herself.

'I'm so sorry. How stupid of me.'

'My dear, I hope you're not scalded.'

Viv took her to the house.

'That's the trouble with tea outside; nowhere to put things,' said Marjorie.

'That's Harriet for you. If it's not one thing it's another,' said the Gunner.

There was an embarrassed silence. Ros stood up with the teapot. 'More tea?'

She refilled two cups and topped up her own. The silence continued. Ros was clear it wasn't the accident that caused the silence, but the comment.

Ros tried: 'I think it's a little cooler.'

'It's the tea, my dear,' said Marjorie, 'that's why they drink it in India – to keep cool. Tea is like thatch: it keeps you warm when it's cold and cool when it's hot.'

'That's curry,' shot the Gunner, 'you've mixed them up.'

To Ros's relief Viv and Miss Beatty weren't long in the house and arrived back. Viv poured Miss Beatty another cup of tea.

The vet drove up the avenue and into the yard. Fred brought him over to the lean-to. 'She's overdue, but it looks like milk fever to me.'

The vet took Dinny's stick and struck her on the hip. She made to rise and couldn't.

'Her far stifle joint is gone. She has no use of that leg.'

'What's to do then?'

'Nothing can be done but save the calf.'

The vet went to the car and took out his bag. He rolled up his sleeve another two turns, put his hand into the cow and slipped it carefully down the side of the calf. He withdrew his hand.

'We won't even do that: the calf is dead. We better take it out what way we can or it might be the knackers instead of the factory to-morrow.'

Viv and Ros tidied the cups and plates onto the trays and left them aside on the grass.

'A delicious tea, my dear. It was every bit as good as one of Mary's,' said Miss Beatty.

Viv smiled and thought: 'The lying old faggot'.

'Was that Fred we saw earlier?'

'Yes, I doubt if you'll see him, he's in trouble with a cow.'

'Men have to work so hard these days, labour is so dear. Ah, here we are.'

A car came up the avenue and stopped opposite the tea party. Viv and Ros helped the two old ladies up, equipped them with walking frame and stick and accompanied them slowly to the car.

'Thank you, my dear.'

'Thank you Vivienne. It was a delightful afternoon despite the heat.'

As Viv and Ros returned to the table the other two were up and ready to go. They walked towards their car with them. Fred saw them coming through the yard and threw some straw over the first bit of the calf on the ground. The vet had his hand inside the cow cutting the next instalment. Fred moved further into the lean-to out of sight. Viv settled Miss Beatty into the passenger seat while Marjorie sat into the driver's seat and started the engine.

'Thank you for a wonderful afternoon.'

She drove out of the yard leaving Viv happy that she had done her duty for another year.

Arthur and Jess

Neither Arthur nor Jess had relatives. It's not unknown for a person in middle age not to have family, but unusual for both of a couple to have no family at all.

Arthur Baker came from Canada. He arrived in Europe with the Canadian Army during World War I and never went back. After the war he came to Ireland with an army friend to his home in Tipperary. There he met Jess, who was English and working nearby as a governess. They married and some years later moved to our town. That was as much as anybody knew about them.

Arthur was at least six feet four, with a shock of grey hair. Like many tall people he walked with a slight stoop. He was a soft, gentle man. He had a long face and when he smiled, as he did often, his mouth withdrew and his lower jaw moved to one side. He was a great romancer. He told stories in the first person that came straight from the *Reader's Digest*.

Jess was small in build, stopping just short of plump. She was no more than up to Arthur's shoulder. She wore crepe-soled shoes and walked with a firm stride. She had a stern face, but when she spoke she looked you straight in the eye and occasionally her face dissolved into a warm smile.

They lived about a mile outside the town in a cottage they had renovated and extended themselves. Arthur was manager of the local newspaper printing-press. He was not a businessman but was a genius with machines. Jess kept house and looked after Muff, their golden cocker. Arthur was fond of the dog too but it was Jess's idea that Muff sleep between them at night. Apart from Arthur's work they weren't involved in anything in the town and they didn't go to church, chapel or meeting house.

When I was a child Arthur and Jess were friends of my parents. In winter they came in at night once every four or five weeks to play bridge and during the summer they occasionally took us to the sea on a Thursday or Sunday afternoon. They had a pre-war *Ford 8*. The men sat in the front; Arthur driving and my father beside him with me on his knee. The ladies sat in the back; my mother and sister, and Jess with Muff on a rug on her knee. It was a squash in the back but if any one had to suffer discomfort it mustn't be Muff.

Arthur and Jess took little notice of us children. One day, however, I met Arthur, by chance, in town. He stopped to talk and to my astonishment he gave me a half-crown; a lot of money for a small boy.

One winter, for no apparent reason, Arthur and Jess stopped coming to our house. They didn't return the invitation to play cards when it was their turn. Eventually Jess called to my mother one afternoon. She confided that Arthur, incredible as it seemed, was having an affair.

Arthur was having an affair with Chrissy. In her early thirties, attractive and capable, she ran the business end of the newspaper. It had been going on for some time before Jess suspected. At first she dismissed it incredulously. Then more and more of the signs pointed the same way until one day she challenged him. Predictably he denied it. He gave reasonable answers to all her questions. She was easily convinced, as she didn't think that Arthur had it in him.

Soon, however, the sinister indicators returned. This time Jess set a trap. She had done her homework and on an evening he was to have been out on business she confronted them both in the dining-room of a country hotel seven or eight miles away.

As she approached, Arthur stood up.

'We had business to discuss,' he started.

Jess looked at Chrissy, whose face went so pale Jess thought she would faint. She turned back to Arthur.

'Take all the time you want to talk business and if you come home when you're finished the door will be locked.'

Jess turned and left.

Arthur took Chrissy back and went home to find that Jess, as he expected, was true to her word. He went into town and with much embarrassment booked into a hotel.

Next morning he phoned home from work and there was no reply. At lunch-time he drove out but found the house empty; no sign of Jess or Muff. He put some things in a bag and went to find his chequebook. All of their personal papers were gone. When he arrived back to work there was a letter that had been delivered by hand. Arthur went into his office, closed the door and read:

Dear Arthur,

You have consistently lied to me for many months now. I have not yet decided what to do. Do not come near the house or try to contact me until I write to you again. – Jess

61

He sat back in his chair and, like a drowning man, his whole life came before him in a flash. He knew that Jess would work things out carefully and that his best hope was to do as she said. He also knew that there was no future for him with Chrissy, not that there ever had been. For both of them the attraction was forbidden fruit. He tried to convince himself that he and Jess had shared so much she would have him back. He oscillated between believing that she needed him too much and knowing that Jess could survive very well on her own. The thought that he might have to survive on his own appalled him.

He was glad it was over. Arthur felt a great relief and kept rehearsing in his mind how he would tell Jess that he had wanted to end it; but the contents of the letter kept coming back to him – Jess had said nothing about the affair, her accusation was that he had consistently lied. He knew that for Jess the lies were the greater sin and there was no way he could mitigate that.

Two days passed. Arthur thought of writing a note just to say sorry but since Jess had said in the letter not to, he decided against it. He knew that he had no option but to wait. He felt the anxiety of a schoolboy who had been found out and was waiting to hear his punishment.

The next day was Friday. The thought of spending the week-end living out of a bag, on his own and without work depressed him, but when he arrived back to his office after lunch there was letter from Jess telling him he could come home.

Arthur was right, it was the lies that were the problem. The irony is that if he had told her the truth she would have found it hard to believe.

Slowly things healed and life returned to normal. The bridge evenings started again.

About a year later my father was transferred and we moved to Dublin. For a few years we exchanged Christmas cards with the Bakers and then lost touch.

I was back a number of times in my late teens and early twenties but the Bakers never entered my head. My parents, who spoke fondly of them when their name came up, didn't enquire.

Shortly after I was married I was back, showing my wife around the town of my birth and the haunts of my youth. I remembered the Bakers and assumed they were dead. They were older than my parents and if alive would be in their late eighties or early nineties.

We drove around by their cottage and parked up the road a little way. It was badly in need of a coat of paint. The garden had been let go and the gravel path was covered with weeds.

As we looked the stooped figure of a man raised his head from under the bonnet of a car at the side of the house and straightened his back. He was wearing a cap. 'It couldn't be,' I said. 'If Arthur is alive, he's not still tinkering with cars?'

I approached, and it wasn't until I was within a few feet that I thought it might be.

'I'm looking for a Mr Baker.'

'Yep, that's me.' I recognised the slight Canadian intonation. I said my name, and he knew immediately.

'Well, it's a long time since I've seen you.'

He was thinner and bent over a little further. He smiled his characteristic smile and said:

'Come in, Jess will be glad to see you.' It was hard to believe that she too was alive. She was even older than Arthur.

I introduced my wife and he led the way into the kitchen, which was smaller than I remembered it. There was Jess, a small frail figure stooped over a stick, trying to manoeuvre between the cooker and a chair.

'Do you know who this is?' Arthur asked.

'I don't play guessing games,' she said, as she broke her journey and sat on the chair. She looked up and before I could tell her she said my name. They were both pleased to see us but we didn't stay long as it was lunch-time.

About two years later I was in town again on business. I called and found that the house was closed up. A neighbour told me they had both had a bad 'flu the previous winter and had been moved to the geriatric hospital and wouldn't be back.

I enquired at the desk. The girl gave me ward numbers on two different floors. I came to the female floor first and asked for Jess. It was a large ward with twelve or fourteen beds. There was a smell of urine masked by disinfectant. Jess was in bed with the cot sides up. She was even smaller than last time. Before I had time to speak she opened her eyes wide and said: 'Did you hear about Arthur?'

'No,' I said.

'He's run away with a nurse.'

'Oh!' I said, and tried to tell her who I was. She lay back and didn't respond.

'I don't think she'll know you,' a passing nurse said.

I went to the next landing and found Arthur in a ward not quite so big. He was sitting out beside his bed in his dressing-gown, dishevelled, and with his pyjama bottoms around his knees. He was in a state of agitation. He looked at me when I spoke and looked away. He couldn't keep still. I spoke again and made no impression. I waited a minute or two, tried once more without success and left.

About two months later I saw the death notice of Jess in the paper. She was buried back in Tipperary where they had lived before they came to our town. I went to the funeral and arrived late. There were five mourners: two neighbours who travelled with the hearse, the son of Arthur's army friend and his wife and myself. I helped to lower the coffin into the grave, which had a neglected headstone on which I deciphered the inscription:

"Arthur William, 'Billy', son of Arthur and Jessica Baker, aged 9 years."

Jim

It was a fine June day; the first real warmth of summer. The car nosed its way slowly along the narrow road with the grass line in the centre brushing the underside. Mary drove carefully manoeuvring around the potholes, occasionally almost stopping to avoid damaging the car. It was heavily weighted in the boot and on the back seat with holiday luggage. In the passenger seat Mary's father watched every inch of the road; a new gate here, Seamus O'Sullivan has gone over to silage; the son has finally won out, Paddy Conlon has put up a lean-to on the shed. There was always something to notice since last year. They arrived at the top of the hill and looked down on the long finger of peninsula pointing out into the Atlantic. Through the haze the horizon was indistinct; a good sign for the weather. This was the moment when Mary's father finally admitted he was on holiday.

The road took them away to the right between sparse hedges and low stonewalls with thorn trees scalded on the windward side. They arrived at the lane to the cottage to find the gate open, and drove up. The hedges on either side had been breasted and the line of grass up the middle had been cut. The door of the cottage was ajar, and every window open. There was a stack of freshly chopped logs in the open shed and the semi-dilapidated garden seat had been painted. Bridie and Paddy had prepared the place for the

Doctor's holiday, as they had done every year for the last sixteen years and as Paddy's mother had done for many years before that. Mary with her mother and father and brother and sister never missed a year here as long as she could remember. She had come with her father and sister since her mother died and alone with her father since her sister was married. She was the youngest and was now working in the practice.

Mary pulled up to the door and went around to let her father out. He was stiff after the long journey but she noticed that he was slowing up recently and she had to help him out of the car.

'Where else could a body want to be?' he said as he stretched his legs and walked over to smell the old-fashioned rose beside the door. Mary took a bag off the back seat and went into the cottage. As she expected: it was spotless. On the table there was an enamel can of milk, a bowl of eggs and a square of brown bread. When she went outside again to unpack the car, Paddy arrived.

'Hello Doctor, hello Mary, did ye have a good journey?'

'We did, thank you Paddy, and how is Bridie and all the family?' Mary enquired.

'The besht. Ye'll have the weather for yeer holiday.'

'Have you had this for long?' the Doctor asked.

'Two days, and it's set. I have the boat ready; will you come out in the evening?'

'I certainly will.'

'How is Jim?' Mary enquired.

'He's fine, the Mammy has him told for a week that ye're coming today, and he has her tormented to know what time ye'd be here. No doubt he'll be up in short.'

Bridie and Paddy had eight children and Jim was the third youngest. He was ten now and two summers ago he took to Mary and followed her around for most of the holiday without saying much. Each time they came since he didn't forget her and spent as much time as he could around the house doing jobs and messages. Mary had become fond of Jim but he never presumed; he always waited to be asked. She took him for walks and out in the car, and talked to him about nature and the sea. He was bright and in his reticent way asked thoughtful questions. He was company for Mary when her father was snoozing or fishing and she was looking forward to seeing him.

Paddy left Mary and the Doctor and went to the shed to tidy up the last few logs and put away the axe.

Mary was pouring a cup of tea for her father when she heard a gentle knock on the open door. There stood Jim.

'Hello,' he said. 'I knew ye were coming.'

He was wearing a tartan shirt, too big for him, and jeans, his hair already starting to bleach.

'Hello Jim. My, you've grown.'

He smiled. Mary ruffled his hair, put her arm around his shoulder and led him into the kitchen. Mary's father greeted him warmly and repeated her comment:

'You've grown.'

'Would you like a cup of tea? I have nothing else until I go to the shop. Would you like to go to the shop yourself?' Mary asked.

'No thanks, I'm grand.'

Mary poured herself a cup of tea and sat down. Jim stayed standing.

'They're after destroying the hedge of honeysuckle below at Conlon's lane. They had a digger in to widen the entrance.'

'Is it all gone?' Mary asked.

'No there's a bit of it left.'

'When I finish unpacking we'll go and have a look.'

Jim helped Mary to empty the car and waited in the kitchen until she came downstairs. The Doctor had settled into a deckchair at the front of the cottage and Mary and Jim set off down the lane.

'How is school?' she asked.

'There's no school, we're on our holidays.'

'I know, but how was it since I saw you last?'

'OK' Jim replied. He didn't want to talk about school but was looking forward to his walk with Mary and listening to her talk about the weather, the seasons, the hedges and the wild flowers. They came to Conlon's and found as Jim had said. About three quarters of the finest stretch of honeysuckle hedge in the area had gone.

'That's very sad,' said Mary. 'And the saddest thing is not that we will miss it, but that whoever destroyed it didn't know what they were doing.'

'Maybe they did and didn't care,' said Jim.

'Maybe that's it.' said Mary, feeling pleased that Jim had learned so much.

They walked on to the harbour where the breeze from the sea tempered the heat. The boats were all out. They walked along the path across the headland and back to the cottage. The Doctor was assembling his rod and sorting out his fishing gear.

'I want to bring the milk can and bowl back to your mother,' Mary said.

'Sure I'll bring them when I'm going.'

'I want to thank her, and anyway I'd like to see her, to see how she is.'

Mary washed the can and the bowl and leaving Jim behind helping her father with his fishing gear she went to see Bridie.

Mary, as usual, had a great welcome and in response to her enquiries an account of all the family.

'I hope that Jim won't be annoying you and the Doctor,' said Bridie. 'He couldn't wait and was like a yo-yo all day going up to see if you were there.'

'Jim is no trouble,' said Mary. 'We both love him around the place. In fact he's a great help and good company.'

'He's the odd one out here,' said Bridie. 'He'll kick football all right but he'd prefer to read. He has the books from the school library read out and has me tormented going to the library when I go to town. Be sure to run him if he gets in the way.'

When Mary arrived back to the cottage Jim was winding line onto a reel for her father who was holding the other end. Mary went inside and set the table for three.

During the holiday Jim never missed a day at the cottage. He would arrive after breakfast and was outside pottering around until Mary came out. He went with her wherever she went during the day and went home around nine, a deadline set by Bridie. Mary was as pleased with his company as ever. He had a knack of fitting in and was sensitive even to the Doctor's little ways and they were both taken by how bright he was and interested in everything that went on.

At breakfast on the morning before they were due to leave Mary asked her father:

'If Paddy and Bridie were to agree, would you mind if Jim came home with us and went to school at St Dominic's, he's old enough to go into the prep department?'

'I hadn't thought of anything like that,' replied her father, 'but I'll leave it to you. Come to think of it, it's a good idea, if his parents agree. The responsibility would fall on you and Teresa. Would Teresa be able to manage when you're on duty?'

'Of course she would. Hadn't she six of her own?' Mary and her father discussed the proposal in great detail and Mary went to see Bridie. She found her at the tap in the yard washing a bucket.

'It'd be all right with Jim, to be sure, he'd follow you to the end of the earth,' was her initial response. 'Are you serious?' asked Bridie.

'I am,' said Mary.

'Well, come inside till we have a cup of tea.'

Bridie led the way into the kitchen and lifting the cover on the cooker she slid the kettle across.

'Mary,' said Bridie, 'you don't mind me asking, but why would you want to do this?'

'Two reasons,' replied Mary. 'The first is that my father and I are both fond of Jim and would like to have him in the house. The second is that he's bright and loves books, and living in a town he'd have easy access to a public library and things in school that he hasn't in the country.'

'I know he has the brains, and I'm not able to keep the books to him, for I only get to town once in a while. You'd be doing him a great honour.' After a pause she added: 'as far as I'm concerned he can go if it's all right with Paddy.'

Paddy made no objection. Mary put the proposition to Jim when she arrived back to the cottage. He gave an uncharacteristic display of excitement and said:

'Will I be coming with you to-morrow?'

Plans were laid for Jim to travel later on, in good time to settle in and find his way around before school started. The Doctor and Mary left the following day. Mary was quietly excited at the prospect of Jim coming late in the summer; she could think of nothing else on the journey home. She went over in her mind the reasons she gave Bridie: that she and her father were both fond of Jim and that it was a pity not to let him have as good an education as possible. She hoped that Jim or Bridie and Paddy wouldn't have second thoughts. She planned his room, his uniform and daily routine and went over in her mind who she might ask in to play with him after school and at week-ends when she was on duty. She knew that she couldn't fill all his boyish needs and that it would be bad for him to spend too much of his time with adults.

The day arrived. Mary drove to Dublin to meet Jim from the train. For the first time she had feelings of apprehension, as much for him as for herself. She imagined how he felt on the train, away from home on his own for the first time. She was also afraid how she would cope if he was homesick; it would be worse for Jim to have tried and failed than not to have tried at all. From her point of view she would have done her best. The mixture of motives and needs of both of them became clearer to her.

The train arrived, the crowd thinned and there he was, with the ticket collector. His face broke into a gentle smile when he saw her.

'Hello Jim.'

'Hello Mary.' She was pleased he used her name. His bag was brand new, as were his shirt, his navy jumper, his jeans and black shoes. She felt sorry for the discomfort he must have felt dressed up, and how the others would have teased him before he left. She thanked the ticket collector, put her arm around Jim's shoulder and went towards the car. Jim took in everything around him, and Mary slipped into telling him things and explaining just like on their walks across the fields and by the sea. She was conscious how new everything was for him here, and on the journey out of the city she stopped herself pointing out things, not to saturate him.

As they drove up the avenue Jim was in awe at the extent of the grounds around the house. The Doctor met them at the door: 'my, Jim, you're looking smart.'

'He's had a long journey and must be hungry' said Mary and brought Jim upstairs to his room, which had been the bedroom of her brother Tom until he went away.

'You might like to change out of your good clothes, and then come down to the kitchen,' Mary said as she left him.

Jim sat on the bed and looked around the room. He couldn't believe that he would have a room this size all to himself. His eye fell on the bookcase and he went to have a look. He changed into his next best clothes, which had been his Sunday best until his most recent outfit, and went downstairs. He was lost in the big house until he heard Mary calling him from the kitchen where she had sandwiches, biscuits and Coke ready.

There were four days before school started; enough time for Jim to find his way around the house and the town and his route to school. Teresa, the housekeeper, who was always there when Mary was on duty, chatted easily to Jim and put him at his ease.

For the first couple of weeks Jim absorbed everything and said little. He watched and waited. Mary brought him to school on the first day. She had second thoughts about arranging for him to meet some boys beforehand, believing that he would have to make his own friends, which he did. By the end of the second week he was talking about Ray, and was soon asked to Ray's house to play after school and Mary encouraged Jim to invite him back. A routine became established. Jim in the house didn't interfere at all with the Doctor, the privacy of whose study he instinctively respected. Mary helped him to acclimatize to the new routine and Teresa looked after the practicalities and set the boundaries when Jim and Ray became too expansive.

The first term went quickly. He had one bout of homesickness but it passed after a few days and Mary insisted that Jim write home, no matter how short a letter, once a week. Bridie wrote back occasionally. At Christmas Jim went home. He was looking forward to it, but the thing he found most difficult was sharing a bed and a bedroom with two of his brothers. He was wise enough not to comment as his brothers and sisters teased him already about his posh school and his 'uppity' ways. Jim did not affect these ways; they were necessary to adapt to his new way of life. He had learned to cope with teasing even before he went away. In his first term Jim had done well at school; he was third in his class at the Christmas exams and his report was good. Although he played football he didn't get on any of the teams and his conduct was 'excellent'.

Mary and the Doctor were glad to see Jim back after Christmas, and he was glad to be back to his room and a bed to himself. For the few days before school started he and Ray spent their time playing between Ray's house and what had now become Jim's. The school routine started again and Jim's Christmas marks and report gave him confidence in his work. When he came in from school he would have a snack and go to his room to do his homework. Only occasionally did he ask Mary for help.

The next 'first' was the summer holidays. It was decided that Jim would stay with Mary and the Doctor until they were going to the cottage and then stay on at home after they left, until just before school in September. Jim knew he would miss Ray and didn't look forward to the cramped accommodation and the teasing from the others. Already at Christmas they had started calling him 'the professor'. He knew the only way to counter it was to ignore it and get stuck into the rough and tumble as best he could. For the first time since he left he looked forward to going home. Somehow distance had drawn him closer to his mother and he looked forward to her occasional letters. Jim's mind raced ahead. He enjoyed being in on that part of Mary and the Doctor's holiday he had never experienced before; the packing of the car and the journey. He was fascinated by their conversation about the things they looked forward to and the expectation of escape from their routine amidst the routine of his own family and their neighbours.

The journey was long and hot with a break to have Teresa's packed lunch. Arriving in the late afternoon he had a strange sensation of divided loyalty as he took his bags and went home. As usual he spent his time between the two cottages as long as the Doctor and Mary were there and he stayed on at home when they went back. This time home he had long conversations with his mother and told her about school and Ray and living with the Doctor and Mary. She was happy that he had the chance and was taking it so well and didn't loose an opportunity to tell him what he owed to the Doctor and Mary. His father said little. He said little to any of his children, but he had such regard for the Doctor Jim knew he must be pleased with the arrangement. Jim was back in time for the new school year and was looking forward to it. He was going into the Senior School a year ahead of his age but was well able for it.

As the years passed Jim became more confident. He understood what the Doctor and Mary were doing for him and in his own way he tried to show his appreciation. His friendship with Ray was as firm as ever. One day Mary overheard them talking about girls from the convent that they passed on their way home from school. When it came to the Inter, Jim's results were excellent. Now he had to choose his subjects for the Leaving. He was diffident when discussing this with Mary, as he wasn't sure that the arrangement included planning for university. Mary left him in no doubt that it did and was thrilled when Jim said: 'thank you very much, would it be all right if I did medicine?' Mary hugged him for the first time. He was embarrassed and blushed, but was pleased she was so happy.

'I hear good news of what you want to do,' the Doctor said to Jim later in the day. This too he was glad of as he had little opportunity of pleasing the Doctor, apart from running the odd message.

Jim chose his subjects and worked as hard as ever. Ray, who was good average hoped to do engineering and they planned to go to university together. After Christmas in Jim's last year at school the Doctor died suddenly. Jim was automatically included with the family in all the arrangements at the funeral. After the rest of the family had left he felt sorry for Mary, and spent what time he could with her but his Leaving was in the offing and much as she enjoyed his company she insisted that he didn't neglect his work. Jim broached the subject of university again under the changed circumstances, but Mary insisted without hesitation that her father's death made no difference to that. Jim duly received the points he needed for medical school, to Mary's delight, and Ray had his points for engineering. The following autumn they went together to university and shared digs in Dublin.

His base was still with Mary, but Jim kept contact with his mother by letter, less frequently now that Mary wasn't there to remind him. He was determined to get his pre-med exams first time and kept his head down. Despite work, he enjoyed university life and Dublin. He and Ray never went out during the week but on Saturday nights they went for a few drinks and on to a student dance.

At Christmas Mary and Jim were invited to Mary's sister in England. Mary went but Jim decided to go home for a few days. Bridie was as proud as Punch that Jim was going to be a doctor. The teasing had stopped, and although they didn't let him see it, his brothers and sisters were proud of him too. For those that were still at home it was a boost to their status with the neighbours. He stayed only four days and went back to the digs to study.

In June he passed his exams and was on course for first year medicine. Ray passed his exams too and the two went off to England for the summer to work on a building site to earn some money. Mary assured Jim that it wasn't necessary but he wanted to make some contribution to his fees and his keep. Mary went to the cottage on her own. It was lonely without her father and Jim and she stayed only a week. When she arrived home she phoned her sister in England and went to her for her second week of holiday. Jim was back at the beginning of September with a free month before term started. Mary was delighted to see him. He did some jobs around the house and in her free time Mary began to teach him to play golf. The four weeks passed quickly and on his last night Mary took Jim out for a meal. They both enjoyed it and related well as adults. Mary missed Jim when he went back, and Teresa didn't help by saying at least once a day: 'the place is very quiet without Jim.'

His second year at university began with the same pattern as the first. Lectures, study and Saturday night out. One Saturday night he met for the second time Brenda, a final year economics student he had met briefly at the end of the previous term, and now instead of going out on Saturday nights with Ray he started to go out with Brenda. As the term wore on two, on the face of it, unconnected things began to happen. He became more enamoured of Brenda and less enamoured of medicine. He began to see Brenda more often but neither of them neglected their work as Brenda had finals coming up and Jim owed it to Mary to stick to his studies. By the time the year's exams came round Jim was clear about two things. One was that Brenda was the girl for him; the other was that he had made a mistake taking medicine. He had no problem telling Mary the first, as he had already mentioned Brenda to her, but he was overcome with anxiety when he thought of telling her that he couldn't go on with medicine. Brenda and Jim both sat their exams and then sat down to decide what to do. Brenda already had a job in England to which she would go. Jim would go with her, having first gone home to tell Mary that he wasn't going on with his studies. Jim's nerve failed. He couldn't bring himself to tell Mary face-to-face, so he wrote a long letter telling her his plans and thanking her for everything.

Brenda and Jim were soon engaged and their wedding arranged for the following summer in Brenda's home parish in Dublin, with Ray as best man. An invitation went out to Mary to which she replied to Brenda's parents, regretting she would not be able to attend as she would be on holiday in America. Enclosed with her reply was a letter to Jim, which Brenda's mother forwarded to him.

It read:

Dear Jim,

I am very sorry indeed that I will not be able to attend your wedding.

I will be with my cousin in America. I'm sorry that I cannot be there as nothing would give me greater pleasure than to see you and Brenda married.

I wish you both all the happiness that life can bring and hope that when you have a chance you'll call to see me.

Please tell Brenda I look forward to meeting her.

Your friend,

Mary.

Jim was on his own when he received the letter. When he read it he burst into tears.

Jim and Brenda were married. Bridie and Paddy were there and most of his brothers and sisters. After their honeymoon they went back to England.

One evening the following summer Mary came in tired from surgery, poured herself a drink in the study, kicked off her shoes and put her feet up. She had taken the first sip when the doorbell rang. She sat for a minute and then dragged herself up to answer it. She opened the door and there stood Jim. It took her a second to take it in. He smiled gently.

'Hello, Mary,' and she threw her arms around him. He held her tightly, lifted her off the ground and put her down.

'Where's Brenda?' she asked.

'In the car.'

'Well go and get her while I put on my shoes.'

Jim brought Brenda into the hall.

'Brenda this is Mary.' The two women embraced warmly.

'I feel I already know you,' said Brenda.

Mary brought them in and poured drinks. Jim and Brenda were on their way from the ferry to stay with Bridie and Paddy. Mary insisted they stay the night.

As Mary took from the oven the meal Teresa left for her to adapt it for three of them, Jim said : 'I just passed my chemistry degree in England. They gave me a year's credit for my time in Dublin. I start teaching when we go back.'

'I never doubted you.'

They talked into the small hours of the morning and when Mary was showing them to their room Jim asked: 'do you mind if I show Brenda the room I used to have?'

'Of course I don't mind, and there's a shirt and a couple of odd socks there you didn't know you had. Teresa was right; she said you'd come back for them one day.'

Aunt Frances

Aunt Frances was six feet two inches tall. She was big-boned and of spare build. She wore thick hand-knitted woollen jumpers, corduroy trousers and men's size ten shoes. She had a long narrow face, kept her hair cropped short and rode a motorbike at a time when few women rode further forward than the pillion.

She was my father's older sister and lived by herself in the family home at the other side of town. Our parents went there only when absolutely necessary, and if we children were sent to her on a message we hoped that she wouldn't be in, and if she were we always had an excuse ready as to why we could not stay. She never held a conversation with us. She wasn't interested in our world and what we were doing. She would simply declaim to us:

'Mon cher…' followed by, what for we children was an endless and barely comprehensible spiel lauding France and everything French. Her monologues on the subject bored us so much that when I came to learn French in school I had a serious psychological block.

Aunt Frances was two years older than my father and she was his only sibling. As he grew up she always wanted to join in his games with his friends. When she was in her early teens she announced one day to her parents that she held them entirely responsible for the fact that she was not a boy. They had no idea how to respond and didn't. They saw it as just another of Frances' little eccentricities and believed she would grow out of it. In her early adulthood she converted to Catholicism and must have been the most faithful and loyal Catholic in Ireland that never went to mass.

From time to time Aunt Frances would explode into our house unannounced, and talk incessantly from the moment she entered until the moment she left, barely taking time to draw breath. That nobody was interested in what she said did not deter her as she talked on and on about Joan of Arc, whom we as children had never heard of. Somehow we knew instinctively that this Joan was not somebody who lived locally. Later my mother explained that she was not just talking about Joan of Arc, she *was* Joan of Arc.

Like all children, our parents often embarrassed us in front of our friends. These occasions of embarrassment were nothing compared with how Aunt Frances caused us to shrivel if friends were with us when she called. If we saw her coming we scattered. If she arrived suddenly and we were trapped, she would question us on our knowledge of France, and then proceed to lecture us on some topic; anything from the Revolution to French cooking.

Aunt Frances was highly intelligent, educated and well-travelled. She had a degree in History and according to my mother spoke fluent French. She was a woman, who, if she had lived in the real world, would have been formidable.

When I was fourteen, to the relief of everybody in the family, long threatening came at last. Aunt Frances, after many false starts, finally moved to France. It was not by chance that she moved to the outskirts of Orleans where Joan of Arc had led the French to a notable victory.

Three or four times a year my father received a long epistle from her. These letters were a mixture of fantasy and reality, but all paid testimony to her contentment and her determination never to return to Ireland.

As the years passed her epistles contained less reference to Joan of Arc, and for some reason she referred more and more to Catherine de Medici. It was a slow transition but her fantasy finally underwent a complete metamorphosis. From her letters we gleaned that the attraction of Catherine was that she had been Queen of France, and the mother of three Kings of France and patron and protagonist of French cuisine. Furthermore she had been a significant influence in promoting the St Bartholomew's Eve massacre of the Huguenots. Though not herself an aggressive or violent person, Aunt Frances would have approved of this atrocity in the interest of upholding the One True Faith, to which, in theory, she subscribed. My father refrained from reminding her that Catherine was in fact Italian, but in the circumstances this may have conveniently allowed her to accept her own foreign origin. He felt a duty to keep in touch with Aunt Frances, but he was careful to keep his letters to her as anodyne and uncontroversial as possible.

The whole family felt a certain relief that our fantasist aunt was determined never to return to live in Ireland. A few letters a year was a small price to pay for the peace of mind to know that she would not arrive unannounced and demand attention for the duration of an extended visit.

My father often left her epistles unopened for days until he had time to read them. One morning a letter arrived with a French postmark written in a strange hand. My father opened it immediately; it was from a neighbour of Aunt Frances to say that she had had a heart attack and was in hospital seriously ill. My father felt a family duty to go to see her. He made arrangements and left the following morning. By the time he arrived at the hospital his sister was dead. He made arrangements for her body to be returned to Ireland for burial.

When the coffin arrived he went down to the local undertaker to collect the papers that came with it. He thought he would have a last look at his sad fantasist sister. When the lid was removed there was the body of a man, in the full dress uniform of a French General, complete with medal ribbons and emblems of decorations. The French undertaker had somehow sent the wrong coffin. My father replaced the lid and decided on the instant not to breathe a word to anybody.

In the presence of her brother and his family and a few friends who had remembered Aunt Frances from earlier years, we buried the General with my grandparents in the family grave in the town's public cemetery.

Aunt Frances in death could be said to have achieved her ultimate fantasy. She was buried in a French military cemetery with full military honours, a war hero of France.

The Pass

I hadn't heard from Joe for a long time. He left a message for me to phone back as soon as I came in. As usual I had to hang on until he had a minute to come to the phone. All he said was: 'Can you come on Thursday, after lunch?'

'Yes,' I said.

'OK, see you then,' and he put down the receiver.

As I approached the town along the estuary road I passed the spot where I first met Joe on a summer day some years before. He had a puncture and flagged me down to borrow a wheel brace. He was fiftyish, his face was round with a serious expression. He was heavy but tall enough to carry it. He wore a collar and tie, a cardigan over a pair of baggy grey flannels and sandals. He spoke slowly and with a great economy of words. I'd have bet he was a schoolmaster.

'If you have time when you're in town I'd like you to have a drink.' He gave me the name of a pub, 'The Barrack'. I thanked him and made a non-committal reply.

I didn't take him up on his offer. In fact I forgot all about it but some months later I was in town again and with time to spend. By chance I came upon 'The Barrack' and remembered the puncture. The pub was on a corner with the door set back three or four feet, the overhang supported by a pillar. It was mainly bar with a small snug partitioned off at the far end. It hadn't seen a coat of paint for at least twenty years. There were two customers in the bar: one sitting at a table reading a paper and one sitting sideways on at the counter gazing out over his pint into the middle distance. Neither of them was Joe. As I stood up to the counter, from the snug I heard the slow, deep voice that had invited me here in the first place. I tapped the counter and out from the snug behind the bar came Joe. He was wearing the barman's old-fashioned white apron. He greeted me warmly, glad of the opportunity to repay the debt.

Since that first visit we discovered common ground. I always called when I was in the area and from time to time he would phone, as he had done on this occasion. Joe became my best contact in the south of the county. If he didn't know about it, it didn't happen. He never greeted me by name, but apart from that treated me like any other customer. I always sat up at the bar, if possible at one end or the other, and as soon as he wasn't busy we would talk. First the pleasantries, then a summary of bits and pieces of interest. No matter how important a piece of information he had to give, he would start with the trivia. He didn't enthuse lest my evaluation of his intelligence didn't coincide with his own. In fact his judgement was as good if not better than mine and when he sent for me it was always worth the journey. Our conversation was usually interrupted and he spoke so softly and cryptically I had to concentrate very hard not to lose some vital detail.

I arrived at 'The Barrack'. There were six or eight people in the bar. Joe took my order, gave me my change and I set in to listen. Normally when he gave me directions I could follow them quite easily but this time the spot was so remote I would need someone with local knowledge. With a barely perceptible movement of his head, like a dealer at an auction, he called up my guide and introduced us.

Jim was about sixty, small, average build, with grey hair showing under a mature cap. He wore a wide American-style tie with a white shirt and a double-breasted blue suit-jacket over a shabby pair of brown corduroys. He had thick glasses with tortoiseshell frames, held together at both hinges by sticking plaster. One lens was even thicker than the other. He perked his head to one side as if to look through the better lens and with a reticent smile said, 'Pleased to meet you.' I knew immediately we were going to get on.

The Twin Rock was about fourteen miles away. Jim would bring me as far as the turn to the old quarry where there was a small country pub, and I would leave him there and pick him up on the way back. We finished our drinks and left.

It was half-day and shops were closed. We walked towards the quay, where I had parked the car. It was May and a clear blue sky. Despite an onshore breeze there was warmth in the air. A screech of gulls was crying like banshees over a trawler where crew were dumping offal. A little further out a tern was sitting on the breeze, dipping from time to time to the ruffled surface of the water. The car was like an oven; we opened the windows and set off.

I knew my way until we turned off the main road nine or ten miles out, so I didn't need the help of my guide at first, but the conversation was slow to get going.

'What do you work at?' I asked.

'Nuttin' much these days, the auld sight is gone.' Pause. 'I'm tryin' to get the blind pension.'

'Don't you need to be totally blind to get that?'

'Well I nearly am, so I thought I'd get most of it; but the bloody auld TDs round here are no good. I'm after bein' to more doctors and medicals; I nearly know the charts off be heart.'

Jim would only talk if I started first. After a long silence I said: 'You're not married?' – sure in my mind that he wasn't.

'I am,' he said.

'Have you family?'

'Twelve livin', but there's only three left in the country. The rest is all in England or America. I have one in Australia.' After a pause: 'God, isn't the country in a shockin' state. The last two to go, went to England after Christmas. I do have to laugh when I hear our crowd condemnin' Thatcher when she can provide the jobs and they can't. They can't even afford to give me the blind pension let alone jobs for me children.'

'Times are hard, right enough, but I think things are looking up,' I said, trying to lift the conversation a bit.

'They are, but aren't the young people gone to the divil with drink and drugs and all this sex?'

'You're right,' I said tersely, not wanting to get into that particular area.

We turned off the main road and Jim directed me through a maze of tiny roads; despite his poor sight his navigation was faultless. We climbed steadily on a narrow road that only had room for one car. The may was coming into bloom. Primroses dotted the ditches on both sides in nature's inimitable asymmetry. The signs of spring were well established.

I dropped Jim at the pub and gave him a couple of pounds to punch in the time. I turned up towards the quarry and arrived at a clearing on the right-hand side of the road. I left the car and walked quietly up the road past the quarry gate, as Joe had told me, to a high bank on the left. I climbed the bank and lay on my stomach, surveying the scene. I had a bird's-eye view of the derelict quarry. From cracks in the long-abandoned quarry face to my left, sprouted grasses, gorse and an occasional small tree. The moorland stretching to my right had worked its way back to the bottom of the rock face.

There was absolute stillness. I noted roughly the point on the ground in tall vegetation beyond the quarry face that Joe had described to me. I lifted my binoculars and searched the sky all round. There was no sign of anything. I lay on my back and waited, scouring the bright, clear sky from time to time. At last, after about an hour and many false alarms, I saw the male harrier coming towards the quarry from my right. At first it was little more than a spot; then a recognisable flight pattern.

I slid back down the bank eight or ten feet to the cover of some low gorse and sat back on my haunches. I was aware of my pulse. Keeping my glasses trained on the approaching male, I glanced at the spot on the ground. Too soon. I looked to the incoming bird. I could now see the blue-grey colour and the black wing tips. I glanced to my left again. Still no move.

As the cock came closer, his steady wing-beat slowed. He began to lose height and I could see the prey locked in his powerful talons. Before he was above the mouth of the quarry he started to glide. I turned to look at the spot, tingling with expectancy. There she was, the hen rising from her concealed nesting site towards the cock. With the cock slightly above and ahead she rolled on her back, showing her pure white rump, relief from her overall brown. He dropped the prey. She caught it in a flash in her outstretched talons. Magic. In a split second the pass was complete and the birds parted.

At that instant the crack of a rifle shot shattered the stillness. I saw a sprinkling of feathers come from the cock. The birds flew in opposite directions but I could see from his flight that he was not injured. In seconds both birds dropped and disappeared into the vegetation beyond the quarry face.

I didn't move for what seemed an age. My heart pounded. I became aware that both my knees pained and one of my legs locked in cramp. I slumped down and sat on the bank. It took some time for the pain to abate. I was thrilled and stunned. My first sight of one of the most spectacular happenings in the bird world, the food pass of the hen harrier, had nearly ended in tragedy.

I crept slowly back up the bank and peered out over the top. Everything was as still as when I arrived. I lay quietly for a long time. There was no sound and no sign of anyone. I went back to the car and sat thinking about what to do. There was nothing for me to do except to tell Joe. I turned the car, and switching off the engine, free-wheeled slowly down the lane towards the pub. I thought I might come on the sniper and was half glad that I didn't.

Jim was waiting. He wanted to buy me a drink but I declined. He finished his pint and we left. I hadn't told him the purpose of my mission and I assumed Joe hadn't either. I didn't know if, from Joe's point of view, it was all right for him to know but I couldn't keep it in. Jim listened carefully and when I finished he perked his head to one side, looked up at me and said: 'the gobshites.'

The Legislator

'That fella's not happy until he's talking about sex, and with women what's more.'

Donie lay back in his armchair in the sitting-room of his tastelessly renovated 19th century farmhouse, his stockinged feet stretched on a stool in front. He lifted the newspaper off his legs and held it up between himself and the television. Angela sat in the chair beside him, legs tucked under her watching intently.

'Why shouldn't he? That kind of discussion is a help to a lot of people.'

'It shouldn't be talked about in public.'

'Dirty jokes are OK but a serious discussion is not?'

Donie turned a page of the paper with a flourish.

'What about children? Isn't it a lovely thing to think of children listening to that kind of thing on television.'

'Children learn about what you call "that kind of thing" in school.'

'Destroying their innocence and making them promiscuous before they're out of short pants.'

'That's when you're stuck, forty years ago when boys wore short pants and babies were found under gooseberry bushes.'

'It's a great pity we didn't all stick then, when children had a childhood and you'd be put off Radio Eireann for saying "damn".

There's no rhyme or reason to the kind of dirt that goes out on the airwaves these days. They laughed at Oliver J, God be good to him, when he said there was no sex in Ireland before television. They knew bloody well what he meant and he was right. What do you think of the nuns inside in the convent listening to that kind of talk on television on a Saturday night, or me mother at home.'

'If there's anything new in it for the nuns, I'm sure they're interested, and your mother is probably thinking that if she knew a quarter of it when she was married she'd have been spared a lot of anxiety.'

Donie dropped his hands, crumpling the newspaper on his lap.

'You know I'm not against sex……….'

Angela cut him off.

'You're not much for it either, unless you're having it somewhere else.'

Donie took his feet off the stool and sat erect in the chair.

'I'll ignore that remark. As I was saying you know I'm not against it but where's it all going to end? Contraception, abortion, homosexuality, and even women are at that now. I'll tell you something that maybe you didn't know: they're farming foetuses for experiments in France.'

'And where did you read that?'

'Never mind, I heard it.'

'Well you can hardly blame the lesbians for that.'

The Late Late Show ended and Donie stood up and turned up the sound on the television.

'Shush, till I hear the news headlines.'

The two listened until Donie broke the silence.

'There they are, stirring it up again. Those bloody journalists never leave us politicians alone. Always trying to trip us up or catch us out; imagine the country we'd have if journalists were running it.'

Angela stood up, put on her slippers and went out to the kitchen.

Next morning Angela went to mass with Donie, as she had done every Sunday since he was elected to the Dáil. When the children were young the whole family went together. Donie considered it important for a man in his position to be seen as a family man no matter what. After mass there was always a confab with some of his business or political cronies, while Angela sat in the car and waited. This morning he was longer than usual; Angela was getting cold. She started to walk and was the best part of a mile out the road when Donie caught up.

'You could have waited.'

'I was frozen. What kept you?'

'I was talking to Paschal. We're in trouble with the takeover of the exploration company.'

Angela was surprised, since he never discussed his business ventures with her. He sometimes told her when he made what he called 'a killing', and gave her a couple of hundred pounds to buy something for herself. She always took it, feeling she was entitled to it for all she did. She would have been happier if he occasionally said 'thanks', but it was a word he never used, at least not to her.

'What do you mean you're in trouble?'

'It wasn't done according to the book, and it looks as though there might be an investigation. If it all comes out it could be serious, but we think we can keep it under wraps.'

'Was what you did illegal?'

'Not exactly.'

'What do you mean not exactly? It either was or it wasn't.'

'It's a matter of having privileged information, but that's hard to prove.'

'So it's another case of not whether the thing is right or wrong, but whether it can be proved or not.'

Donie did not reply but fixed an impassive look on his face, and drove the rest of the way home in silence. He went straight to the phone and was still on it when Angela called him for lunch. Even though there were just the two of them now they still used the dining-room for Sunday lunch.

'Who were you talking to on the phone?'

'Michael.'

'Did you tell him?'

'I did.'

Donie blessed himself, said grace before meals and started to carve.

'What did he say?'

'He thought they would find it hard to prove anything, but some of the dirt might stick.'

Angela poured water into the two glasses, and said:

'Maybe you should go back to Lourdes:

"Ah, it's Donie, how have you been since I saw you last?"

"Well, Our Blessed Lady, I'm still off the drink, but I have a spot of bother in business.""

'Stop your blasphemy, and you only after coming from mass. That's the kind of thing has the country in the state it's in – no respect for religion. God be with the days when everyone went to mass and you wouldn't be embarrassed to bring your granny to the pictures.'

'Yes,' said Angela, 'and three quarters of the people lived in holy poverty and blessed ignorance, and sex were what posh people's coal came in.'

'Oh you can jeer all you like but you know in your heart and soul it was a better country then.'

'Better for who? The thousands that had to emigrate or had no jobs, or the women whose function was between the bed and the….'

Donie stood up, banged the table and knocked his chair over behind him.

'Will you shut up and stop tormenting me when I have business problems on my mind, I have to listen to the same old stuff over and…'

'Well you won't have to listen to it much longer.'

'……over again. I'm fed up with it. If that's all you have to say you can hold your tongue for I know it off by heart.'

Donie picked up the chair and sat down. He pulled it in to the table and pushed his plate away. Angela helped herself to more gravy. There was a long silence that Donie broke.

'What do you mean I won't have to put up with it much longer?'

'Just what I said.'

'Why?'

'I'm leaving.'

'What do you mean you're leaving?'

'I'm going.'

'Going where?'

'I'm not sure yet, but I'll let you know when the time comes.'

'For how long?'

'For good.'

'You mean you're leaving?'

'That's what I said.'

Donie pulled back his plate and wiped the potato off the handle of his knife.

'Why?'

'You know why. We haven't had a marriage for the past twenty years.'

'What do you mean? Everything's all right as far as I'm concerned.'

'Well it isn't, as far as I'm concerned.' Angela came back: 'we live under the same roof and that's the end of it.'

'And what do you expect at this stage of our lives?'

'I expect a little consideration; to be treated like a person with a mind and a life of my own and not an unpaid housekeeper and secretary.'

'Well if it's more money you want why didn't you say so?'

Incredulous, Angela opened her mouth and nothing came out. She took a deep breath to stop herself shouting, and controlled carefully her modulation.

'We never had a marriage. When the children were young you were out night and day building what you call your political base. Then you were elected and you had to be out night and day maintaining it, hand-shaking, back-slapping and buying drink for half the country, coming home in the small hours of the morning. Then the drink took over completely and you might or might not come in at all, and when you did you were disgusting; drunk and disgusting.'

'I gave it up, didn't I?'

'You did, but believe it or not you were easier to live with when you were drinking.'

'Well that's a good one; you never let up until I'm off the drink, and now you want me back on it. You make it sound as if you want to leave because I'm off the drink, which doesn't make sense. What do I have to do to get you to stay?'

Angela took some dishes from the table to the kitchen. Donie followed and stood beside her at the worktop and tried to look into her face. If that hadn't irritated her so much she might almost have felt sorry for him. She walked to the far end of the kitchen and turned to face him.

'Look Donie, it would take me a week to explain to you, and even then you wouldn't understand. We're poles apart and we'll never be any other way. We haven't had a marriage for years, and it's time to call it a day.'

'Why didn't you tell me before?'

'How could you not see for yourself? I'm telling you now because I've decided to do something about it.'

'And have I no say in the matter? Is there not something we can do?'

'No Donie, it's too late.'

Angela took the desert on a tray to the dining-room. Donie followed and sat down.

'Where does this leave me?'

'I don't know; just where you are; you won't have to move and you won't have to support me.'

'So there's somebody else.'

Angela was surprised and disappointed; surprised that he allowed himself to think it was possible and disappointed, as she had wanted to tell him.

'And what makes you think I can't support myself?'

'Well is there someone else?'

'Since you put it like that, there is.'

Angela waited for him to lose his temper and bang the table again, but he didn't.

'So the whole countryside knows except me, and they're laughing at the good of it.' He bared his teeth and hissed from between narrowed lips: 'Poor Donie, and he doesn't know the first thing about it.'

He resumed his normal voice and banged the table again.

'Who is it?'

'No one you'd know. He's not from around here.'

'Where's he from?'

'I'm not telling you.'

'And what do you think this is going to do to my political career? I'll be ruined at the polls and in the party.'

'Do you expect me to live the rest of my life in hell for the sake of your career?'

'I gave up the drink didn't I?'

'You did, but bad and all as it was to live with a drunk, to live with a humoursome, self-righteous, holy Joe that takes the high moral ground on every conceivable issue, is a hundred times worse.'

Donie gave no indication that he had heard.

'We'll try for a Church annulment,' he said.

Angela couldn't believe her ears:

'Whatever about your own mental state, you won't get an annulment on the grounds that I'm insane.'

William

There had been tension in the house since Breda started going out with William. Weekends were worst; since that was the time the young couple were able to see each other. Ned and Mary and their three adult daughters all lived at home.

Ned scraped his boots cursorily at the back door; a regulation imposed since Mary had the new tiles laid. He hung his silage-scented coat in the back porch, took off his cap and pushed in the door to the kitchen. A fug of warm air, tinged with the smell of rashers frying, caught his breath.

'You're late,' Mary said expecting him to account for the fact.

'The boss was away all afternoon and I had to feed the calves on my own.'

'Breda wasn't in Dublin at all at the weekend. She was up North with that fella' again.'

'How do you know?'

'I found the train ticket in her coat pocket.'

Ned made no comment. He and Mary had hoped that Breda's relationship with William would run its course, but it didn't look as if it would. They had been going together now for the best part of a year, and the only thing Mary and Ned knew about him was that he was a Northern Protestant. Although Ned had worked nearly thirty years for a Protestant farmer for whom he had a great respect and loyalty, it was a different matter when his youngest daughter might marry one, especially a Northern one.

Ned wasn't enamoured of the idea, but he wasn't as dead against it as Mary was. He had to express his disfavour to keep on the right side of his wife. He sat to the cooker and took up the paper. Though he wouldn't have admitted it, Breda was his favourite daughter. He couldn't concentrate to read, put down the paper and said to Mary:

'Why don't we ask her to bring him home one weekend? As long as she knows we don't approve she'll stay with him. If he comes here it's a good chance it'll put him off, a Northern Prod in the heart of Catholic Ireland.'

'God she's terrible stubborn.'

'Begod she is,' thought Ned to himself, 'I wonder how that came about?' Mary went on:

'I suppose if she's going to stay with him we'll have to meet him sooner or later, and inviting him down might knock the contrariness out of her, and it might cure him too and if it doesn't we've nothing to lose.'

Breda's relationship with William was not a problem for Lena and Peg, her two older sisters. In fact they conspired with her and spoke up for her to keep the peace in the house. They couldn't have cared less what William's religion was so long as he was a decent fella' and he made Breda happy.

When Breda came in from work the next evening Mary made herself scarce and when Ned and she were alone together in the kitchen Ned broached the subject.

'Why don't you invite that fella' of yours down here some weekend?' There was a long silence, and then:

'Are you serious?'

'Of course I'm serious. Why would I say a thing like that if I wasn't serious?' There was another silence.

'Me Ma'd never agree.'

'She will agree. You're long enough around this house to know I wouldn't make a suggestion like that without talking to your Ma about it first.'

'And she agrees?'

'She does indeed.'

'And if I brought William down here would she be civil to him?'

'Of course she'd be civil to him. Now I wouldn't say she'd be all over him, for you know the difference in religion is a big thing with your mother. It wouldn't be as hard for her to accept if he was a local Protestant but a Northern one is a different kettle of fish.'

'William is a lovely fella' and his family are lovely people. When I go up there they make me welcome.'

'Well, we'll do the same for him when he comes down here.'

'Da, his name is William, you could call him by his name.'

'We'll make William welcome in this house.'

Breda arranged that two weeks later William would come for the weekend. She was delighted but nervous and William tried to put her at her ease. He too was pleased with the development and saw it as the next step on the road to their getting engaged.

'Of course your mother and father aren't over the moon. We live in a terrible bloody country where all that religion stuff comes before people's happiness, but we've agreed we're not going to let it get in our way.'

As the day approached Lena and Peg, who weren't afraid to cross their mother if necessary, painted the picture for Mary and Lena laid it on the line to her.

'William will be a guest in our house and you are to make him welcome, and not just by saying so. We will all be warm and friendly and make him feel at ease and not only for Breda's sake, but because it's the right thing to do, and for God's sake stay off religion,' and with a hint of humour to lighten things, she added, 'and whatever you do don't mention the Pope!' Ned grinned.

As the day approached there was some nervousness all round. When the car arrived into the yard from the station Ned went out; Mary stayed inside.

'Daddy, this is William.'

'You're very welcome to our house,' Ned said, as he put out his hand.

'Pleased to meet you, Mr Neill,' William replied in his strong Northern accent and with his warm smile. In the kitchen Breda repeated the introduction:

'Mammy, this is William.' William went straight over to the cooker:

'I'm pleased to meet you Mrs Neill.' Breda's two sisters came in and gave William a warm welcome.

'You must be hungry,' Mary said, 'sit to the table and we'll have something to eat.'

The six sat to the kitchen table on which Mary had put a cloth for the occasion. There was small talk about the weather and the journey down. Since Breda hadn't been able to talk to her parents about William she had talked to her sisters who knew a good deal about him.

'Did you go straight to sea when you left school?' Peg asked. William smiled.

'If you could call the Stranraer ferry going to sea, I did. I'm home most nights. The sea is in my blood. My father and grandfather were both deep sea, but that's no life for a family. I'm happy the way I am.' Breda smiled across the table at William. Then there was a silence that Breda broke.

'William's Daddy was killed in an accident at sea.'

'God love you,' Mary said, crossing herself.

'How long ago is that?' Lena asked.

'Three years ago.'

'Well I'm sure your Mammy is glad you're not going to sea,' Mary said.

'He *is* at sea,' Breda came in defensively, 'There's sea between Larne and Stranraer.'

Next morning Ned brought William up to the farm to see the cattle that were in the shed for the winter. William was wearing the blue suit that he had worn the previous evening to present the right image to Breda's parents. The cattle were at the silage face. Their breath was condensing on the frosty air and there was a heavy smell of slurry. William was incongruous in his city suit. He picked his way up the shed towards the cattle stepping carefully over straw and

106

dung in his polished cuban-heeled boots. He said something that Ned couldn't understand and so absorbed was Ned in the thought that he had never seen somebody so out of place in his life, he didn't ask him to repeat it. None the less he admired the young man's enthusiasm in agreeing to come to see the cattle. William didn't comment on the smell that must have been stifling for him, nor did he utter a regret that he hadn't taken up Ned's offer of wellington boots before they left the house.

As they approached the silage face Ned picked up the word 'cows' in something William said and found himself explaining to him the whole of the milk and beef systems from bulls through cows, bullocks, heifers and calves. It was all new to William who with his open face and broad smile listened attentively and nodded as though he understood every word.

On Sunday morning Mary and Ned went to mass while the three girls and William went for a walk. The last thing in the world that would have occurred to William was to find out and attend the local Protestant Church. Lena and Peg liked their sister's boyfriend and they hoped that their mother's reserve towards him was not making him feel uncomfortable. Sunday lunch was relaxed with some tentative jokes about North and South. After lunch Lena drove William and Breda to the station and as she waited for Breda to come back from the platform she felt a great relief that over the weekend nobody had said anything untoward.

After William's first visit to Breda's family he and Breda each paid weekend visits to the family of the other, and after about six months they decided they wanted to be engaged. William insisted that they should say nothing to anyone, not even Lena and Peg, until he had asked Ned for Breda's hand in marriage. On the Saturday morning of a visit South Ned informed William that, as the boss was away, he was going up to the farm to look at the cattle, and asked if he would like to continue his agricultural education. This was just the kind of opportunity that William was hoping for. As they crossed the field at the back of the house William decided to ask the question.

'Mr Neill, I want to ask you a question.'

'Go on try me, I've been a lifetime at this farming, but I don't know everything.'

'It's nothing to do with farming,' and William came straight out with it. 'I want to ask you for Breda's hand in marriage.' Ned stopped and looked straight ahead. There was a long silence, such that William's heart sank. Eventually Ned spoke.

'Well merciful hour, I thought that those days were long gone. I thought that young people these days made up their minds and then told their parents, whether they liked it or not. Thank God there's still a bit of old fashioned decency left in the world. I suppose she knows you're going to ask?'

'She does.'

'And I suppose if it's OK with me it's OK with her?'

'It is.'

'Well William, it's like this: it's OK with me, but the question is,' Ned said turning to William with an impish grin, 'which of us is going to tell her mother?' William didn't quite know how to respond to this, and Ned continued, 'don't worry, son, I'll look after that.'

When they arrived back to the house, while Ned was taking off his boots in the back porch, William went into the kitchen. Breda knew from his smile that things had gone well. She took William's hand and led him down to the sittingroom and closed over the door.

She hugged him tightly and said:

'That's the first hurdle over, but the next one might be a problem.'

'Don't worry,' William said, 'your father is going to look after it with your mother.'

'It won't be as easy as that, but since he's made up his mind she'll agree under protest.'

'That'll be good enough for us. That's all we need.'

'She'll insist that we get married in the Catholic Church.'

'We've known that all along,' William said, 'and that's OK with me, and if we can get the local Protestant minister to take part it'll make it easier for my mother.'

Mary did agree, but took the good out of it by showing no enthusiasm, and this prevented Ned from expressing openly his happiness for his favourite daughter. Lena and Peg made up for it. They were delighted and showed it. They both hugged William, and Lena danced around the kitchen with Breda while Mary turned her back and worked away at the cooker. In two weeks William and Breda made their engagement public and began to make plans for the wedding.

The day arrived and there was a good contingent of William's family and friends down from the North. The parish priest was more than helpful to the young couple and the local Protestant minister was happy to take part. Lena and Peg kept an eye on arrangements to be sure that there would be no awkwardness due to the religious and cultural differences. They were glad that custom had it that it was the bride's father that spoke at the reception and not her mother. None the less the sisters, in order to leave nothing to chance, composed and wrote out Ned's speech, and put him on pain of his life to stick to it word for word.

The service went well, but in the circumstances it was impossible that some differences would not be noticed. The main one that a stranger might observe was that for the hymns one side of the church sang lustily while the other side stood mute. Outside Lena and Peg, the two bridesmaids, were pleased; so far so good.

The next difference that became immediately noticeable was when the wedding party arrived at the hotel most of the bride's family and friends made straight for the bar while most of the guests of the groom went into the lounge and ordered tea. Lena and Peg, with William's help, had planned carefully the seating arrangements for the meal, mixing both sets of guests as best they could, but being careful to put likely-to-mix-well with likely-to-mix-well and keeping unlikely people apart.

The meal was good, and when it was over, Ian, William's best man, read the cards and to Lena and Peg's relief there was no vulgarity or even smut. Then he said:

'I now call on Mr Neill to propose the toast to the bride and groom.' Ned, looking every bit the part in his brand new suit, stood up, speech in hand, and went to take his glasses from his top pocket. They weren't there. He tried his two side pockets. They weren't there either. He tried his inside pocket, his trouser pockets and even his back pocket. No glasses. He opened the speech, held it away from him the full length of his arm. He squinted, drew it back and held it out again, then he held it up and, suspiciously unperturbed, he began:

'I have here the speech that Lena and Peg wrote for me, but since I've forgotten my glasses I'll have to do without it,' and he put the piece of paper in his pocket. Lena and Peg froze. Ned went on:

'The first thing I want to say is this: William has been coming down to our house now for over a year. He's a bright and happy young man, always in good form and ready for a joke and bit of fun.' Lena and Peg relaxed. Ned continued:

'We love to see William coming, but the fact of the matter, whether you like it or not, there's a problem.' Ned paused and then continued. 'No matter how hard Mary and I try we can't get over this problem.' Lena put her hands to her head. A wave of nausea coursed through Peg's stomach. Ned continued:

'Now this may not be a problem for some of Breda's family and friends, but it's a problem for her mother and meself. You see, the thing is....' and Ned paused again, '...neither of us can understand the half he says.'

The Home

'Put the chair to the door,' said Paddy. 'I think Head Crow is on to us.'

Ben pulled the chair across and wedged it under the handle of the door while Paddy rummaged at the back of his locker and produced the naggin of whiskey. He poured some into his glass and into a mug for Ben.

'Why do you think she's on to us?'

'She's calling in here more often than is natural with nothing more to say than comment on the weather or to feel the radiator. The auld crow is as cute as a fox.'

They both added water to their whiskey from the tap in the handbasin and sat back, Paddy on the bed and Ben on the easy chair, to indulge their nightly ritual before going down to the sitting-room among the women, to watch the Nine O'Clock News.

Paddy and Ben were by way of an experiment in the home. Sister Angela disturbed by the bitchiness of the old ladies convinced the Order that their behaviour would improve if she took in men, and the Order agreed to try by starting with two. Initially she was pleased with her choice as they worked together from the start. Both widowers in their early eighties, and, fit for their age, they settled in quickly. They sat together at meals and beside each other in the circle in the sitting-room and went out for a walk together in the afternoons. They had separate rooms, which didn't go down well with the ladies who, apart from two or three of them, had to share. As far as improved behaviour was concerned, there was less bickering when the men were there and Paddy's humorous ways lightened the company when he was present. Sister Angela had hoped that they would have mixed more with the ladies but with only two of them she understood.

'Did you see that row at lunch time when Sadie sat in the wrong place; they're a shocking crowd of auld ones,' said Ben.

'Waiting around to die, is all they're doing. They've all given up,' said Paddy. 'Well begod I'm not giving up that easy. There's life in the auld dog yet and he's going to live it to the full, Head Crow or no Head Crow.'

'She's a decent auld skin, all the same,' said Ben. 'Where would all these auld Biddys be without her, and sure where would we be?'

'Without her we'd be able to come and go as we please, and have a smoke when and where we wanted,' said Paddy, 'and we wouldn't be hounded to go to that chapel against our will. Religion is a matter for free conscience, but for her belief in God is compulsory. Do you believe in God?'

'Of course I do,' replied Ben. 'Didn't I believe in him all me life?'

'Well do you believe in him now after being in here and seeing all these auld ones at different stages of decay?'

There was a knock and the door was pushed forward into the chair that jammed it. Paddy grabbed the naggin and Ben's mug and put them with his glass into the locker.

'Just a minute Sister,' he said. 'The chair is in the way.'

He moved the chair and standing back opened the door to Sister Angela.

'I don't think it's a good idea to spend so much time in your room,' she said. 'You should spend more time with the ladies.'

'We're both a bit shy, Sister' said Paddy, 'and we're not very good at the knittin'.'

'They like your company, you know,' she said.

'Well that doesn't surprise you now, Sister,' said Paddy. 'Two fine young fellows like us, but we're afraid of being the means of them puttin' immoral thoughts in their minds and puttin' their immortal souls in danger. When we're there you'd never know what they'd be thinking, but we'll be going down for the news in a few minutes.'

'Is the new ferule on your stick an improvement?' she asked Ben, ignoring Paddy's comments. 'You need to be careful on the tiles in the hall.'

She went, leaving the door open behind her. When he heard her footsteps on the stairs Paddy closed the door gently.

'I told you she was onto us,' he said, as he took the drinks out of the locker.

They knocked back the whiskey, swilled out the glass and the mug and went downstairs to the sitting-room.

The room was large and oblong with the television in the bay window at the far end from the door. The room was over-heated and stuffy, the carpet was shabby, and there were two large reproduction pictures on the walls. A row of assorted chairs lined the room. Every chair was filled except for theirs, every woman sitting in her own chair. Some were reading, one or two knitting or sewing, most just sitting and staring ahead and two of them were in a twilight zone as though they'd had a knockout punch from a heavyweight boxer.

Paddy and Ben took their places in the circle and watched the ads. It wasn't that the Nine O'Clock News was compulsory but cocoa and biscuits arrived after the weather forecast and the nurses helped those that needed help to their rooms. Paddy and Ben were both smokers and the only time they were allowed to smoke in the sitting-room was when all the women had gone to bed.

The news began but no more than two or three of the women took any notice.

'There's no good news these days,' one of them said.

'There never was and there never will be,' said Paddy. 'You have to make your own good news, and if you don't, no one will.' No response. A nurse came in and put a tray with mugs and biscuits on the table in the centre of the room. The news droned on with pictures of rioting in the Middle East. The nurse returned with a big jug of cocoa. The news ended and the weather forecast began. The sprightly Mrs Martin who always poured the cocoa went to the table and two others handed around the cocoa and biscuits. Some of them didn't take it and others had to wait till the nurse came back to help. Neither Paddy nor Ben took cocoa; they were waiting for them all to be gone to have the place to themselves for a smoke.

One by one they drifted off to bed, the nurse helping the feeble ones. Paddy changed the channel and looked around impatiently. There was only one left, and she was asleep.

'Get up owa that and go on to your bed till we have a bit o' peace and a smoke,' Paddy said under his breath. Ben coughed and banged the arm of his chair.

'She knows bleddy well. She's trying to torment us,' said Paddy.

The nurse came back for the tray. 'Are you not in bed yet Mrs Kelly?' There was no response. The nurse went over and shook her 'Mrs Kelly it's time for bed.' The old woman fell forward. The nurse could find no pulse.

'Give me a hand, Paddy,' the nurse said calmly as she laid her gently on the floor.

'Begod there'll be no smoke to-night,' said Ben as he picked up his stick and made for the door.

The Festival

Ned banged the table and called the meeting to order. It was ten past eight and there were more committee members to come, but he never gave them more than ten minutes' grace. The ones in the bar drifted in with their pints; attendance at committee meetings had improved since they began to hold them in Clancy's back room. The Festival committee was composed of representatives of every organization in the village. The same people had served for the four years of its existence and had run four successful festivals; this was the first meeting to plan the fifth.

Gartmore was a village of about 120 people, one shop, a post office, two pubs, a garage, a school, a parish hall and a church. It served a hinterland of small hill-farmers and if strangers were seen in the village it was certain they were lost. The county town was seven miles away and not more than a half dozen of its inhabitants, if they knew of Gartmore's existence, would have known how to find it. It was more like an English village, in that there was a triangular green in the centre around which the whole village was ranged and the uninteresting countryside rose on two sides to small farms and wooded hills beyond. On the third side was the principal road into the village that connected, via other small roads, with a main route five miles away. The Festival which had been Father

Ryan, the curate's, idea had drawn on the village's community spirit and developed it into a lively community pride.

Ned Downey, who owned the garage, had been chairman from the beginning, and he called tonight's meeting to make those arrangements that needed to be made well in advance. When the band for the marquee dance had been agreed and the printing and publicity planned, Ned came to the principal decision of the evening:

'Now ladies and gentlemen,' he said, 'who are we going to ask to open the Festival this year? We're running out of local notables; we've had the parish priest, the rector, our own county councillor and the assistant county engineer. We'll have to look further afield. Any suggestions?' There was a long silence.

'Would we ask a county councillor from one of the other parties?' someone suggested.

'We asked Eddie because he lives in the village,' replied Ned. 'If we do that we'll have to have one from every party, and where would we draw the line?'

'What about the principal from the school?' asked someone.

'What about her?' said someone else, and there was an awkward silence.

'Why don't we ask the President?' suggested Delia, the ICA representative.

'The President of what?' someone asked.

'The President of Ireland.' A few people laughed.

'I'm serious,' said Delia. 'She said she was going to be a President for the people, and she'd be turning up in the most unlikely places. She'll never turn up in a more unlikely place than Gartmore and it's certain she won't turn up here if we don't ask her.'

'We certainly qualify under the heading of "the most unlikely places",' said Billy of the GAA. 'She's probably never heard of Gartmore.'

'Be the jizzes,' said Paddy who never started to say something without that particular preface and who didn't represent anybody but himself, 'I've a better idea. Why don't we ask the Pope?' Everybody laughed. Ned called the meeting to order.

'Delia's right,' he said, 'it's worth a try, she can only say no.'

'Maybe we should think of her for next year,' said Billy, 'when we see what kind of places she goes to.'

'Why can't we set the trend?' asked Delia. 'Ned's right, she can only say no.'

'There's no harm in asking,' said Billy. 'But we shouldn't tell anybody until we hear from her, they'll make a right jeer of us if she doesn't come.'

'I think we should ask her,' said Ned, 'we've nothing to lose, we're only taking her at her word.'

The committee agreed and Delia, who was secretary, was asked to write to the President.

'I think that's all for tonight,' said Ned and closed the meeting.

No decision was made to keep the matter within the committee as everybody knew there was no point; confidentiality in Gartmore, as in every other village in the country was a matter of telling only one person at a time. The committee's invitation to the President generated great interest and diverse opinions. Some people felt a great sense of expectation and others thought the committee had made a laughing-stock of itself and the whole village.

A week to the day Delia called to Downey's garage to look for Ned. She was in a state of high excitement and found two feet sticking out from under a car. She bent down and looked underneath.

'Ned,' she said, 'come out for a minute till I tell you.' Ned slid out and could see that Delia was uncharacteristically flustered.

'Is she going to come?' he asked.

'No, but her secretary has just been on the phone to ask for more details; what's involved and a whole lot of questions about the committee and the village. I asked her how soon we would know, and she said she couldn't say, but she'd give the information to the President.'

'That looks hopeful,' said Ned, 'and it'll be one-in-the-eye for the begrudgers.'

'I don't know how great it'll be,' said Delia, 'I'm a bag of nerves as it is.'

'Have you told anyone else?' asked Ned.

'No.'

'Well don't until we hear. We'll keep it between the two of us.'

One day the following week there was an official envelope in the post for Delia. When she saw it on the floor her stomach turned over. She didn't know whether she wanted it to be 'yes' or 'no'. She opened the envelope and read. All she could see was 'The President has much pleasure in accepting.......' She sat down and read the letter through. The President was coming. She checked her hair in the mirror without seeing it, put on her coat and went down to the garage. Ned was with a man in the office and after what seemed like an age he came out. She handed him the letter without a word.

The whole village knew by lunchtime and, apart from a few hardened begrudgers, people were pleased, if a little anxious that they would not let themselves down. They knew that the whole countryside would be watching and it would be hard work to make it an event worthy of a visit from the President.

Ned called a meeting of the committee right away to lay plans for the visit of their distinguished guest. The one thing they were determined on was that the opening itself would be longer and more elaborate than usual. Ned had already spoken to Father Ryan who volunteered his dining-room for dinner after the ceremony so the President would be in the village for the whole evening to make it worth her while coming.

As spring emerged slowly from the greyness of winter there were signs of beautification in Gartmore further to nature's annual display. There were houses painted that hadn't seen a lick of paint in living memory. The Tidy Towns Committee put new flower-beds on two sides of the green and the County Council re-surfaced the street the whole way around the green and half-a-mile out the road. Ned painted up the garage and had the wrecks taken away from the side and the back, and the shop and post office both put wastepaper boxes at their doors. By early summer Gartmore was sparkling.

The week before the Festival the village was abuzz. Father Ryan, who when it came to it was the most excitable of them all, resorted under pressure to the odd glass of whiskey. He rowed in with the committee in making plans and doing what had to be done. There were reporters looking for interviews and the Special Branch, guided by the local Guard, surveyed the village. Ned gave them details of the opening and they went through Father Ryan's house from top to bottom. Everything was put in place and the committee was satisfied that they had done all they could.

The day arrived. The big talking point was the weather; it looked as if, at best, it would be dull with showers. By evening the village was a showpiece; bunting everywhere, and anyone who had a flag, National, Papal, GAA or any other kind, hung it out. There was a new flagpole for the National flag on the green and beside it a lorry trailer as a platform for the VIPs with chairs and a microphone. The band arrived early and sat below the trailer. They began to practise. Children played around the green, acting to the tunes of the band. Somebody tested the amplification. The Irish dancers arrived and the mothers examined the platform beyond the band where they would dance. People came from all parts and soon there was a crowd around the green. Extra Guards had been drafted in directed by a superintendent. At a quarter to eight Ned and the committee, with Father Ryan and the other VIPs positioned themselves on the edge of the green at the approach road. The superintendent told them she would be on time. The sky was threatening but the rain held off and at two minutes to eight a buzz went through the crowd as the motorbike escort followed by the presidential car came around the bend of the road and was visible from the village. The nerves in Ned's stomach tightened as the car stopped in front of him. The driver opened the door and the President stood out. The band, on cue, played the presidential salute, at the end of which Ned stepped forward and the President put out her hand and smiled.

'Welcome to Gartmore, your Excellency,' Ned said as they shook hands.

'I'm delighted to be here,' she replied. 'Thank you for asking me.' Ned introduced her to the rest of the VIPs and led her across the green to the trailer. One of the committee members hopped up on the trailer from the side to help her up from the top of the steps, which, since she was wearing a tight skirt, she negotiated with great difficulty.

'That's a mistake I won't make again!' said the President, laughing.

Father Ryan, who by this time was highly excited, made sure everyone was in their right seat and signalled frantically to Ned, who was in relaxed conversation with the President, to start. Ned stood forward and said:

'Your Excellency…..' and realized the microphone was dead. Father Ryan leaped up and turned on the switch. 'Your Excellency, on behalf of all the people of Gartmore I bid you céad míle fáilte' and the crowd broke into prolonged applause. 'You have done us a great honour in coming to our Festival this year…' More applause. Ned delivered a short and appropriate speech from his carefully prepared notes and before sitting down called on Father Ryan to say a few words. Father Ryan stepped forward and pitching his voice as if there were no microphone and he wanted to be heard in the next county, began: 'Tá áthas mór orm……..' and went on in Irish for a good five minutes. Just when everybody was beginning to feel uncomfortable he broke into English, which relieved the situation slightly but by the time he was on his feet for more than ten minutes it became clear that, like a runaway horse, he didn't know how to stop. Eventually he did and sat down exhausted. Ned then asked the Rector to say a few words. As the Rector stepped forward Father Ryan, who was a good friend, whispered: 'Good man Bill, and keep it short'. The Rector welcomed the President, thanked her for coming, wished her well in her Presidency and sat down. Ned then called on the President to open the Festival officially. There was another round of applause and the President began. She thanked the committee for asking her to come, and made it plain that Gartmore had done her an honour rather than the other way round. They were first to take her at her word and invite her to such an event.

'The most important place in the country for all of you is Gartmore,' she said, 'and it is fitting that the President should open a festival in the most important place in Ireland.' There was a great cheer and prolonged clapping. She showed interest and gave encouragement in everything she said and by the time she had finished everybody was entirely at ease except Father Ryan. He then introduced the Irish dancers to perform for the President. When all the formalities were over, Father Ryan and Ned showed the

President around the village. She stopped frequently to talk to the people.

As the events of the evening proceeded the night became chilly so the President, the VIPs and the committee retired to Father Ryan's house for the big meal, provided by his housekeeper and the members of the ICA. Father Ryan presided at the top of the table with the President on his right. There was no danger of a lapse in the conversation now that he had relaxed with the help of a few glasses of whiskey.

The President remarked how fortunate it was that the weather held up, to which Father Ryan replied; 'You needn't have worried at all about the weather, the Holy Spirit and myself had that arranged.'

'At least he put the Holy Spirit first,' Delia whispered to Billy.

The conversation flowed easily, as did the whiskey and the meal was superb. There were so many helpers and so much food there were offers to replace every forkful eaten. At the first short silence in the conversation Paddy spoke up.

'Be the jizzes, Mrs President, you're the great woman to come to Gartmore. I never thought I'd see the day when I'd be atin' me dinner at the same table as the President of Ireland. It's a great honour for me, and I'm only sorry me mother and father didn't live to see it.'

'Thank you, Paddy,' Father Ryan interjected, afraid of what he would say next, and turning to the President added: 'That, Madam President, is Paddy Fagan, a substantial farmer from these parts. He's nearly fifty years of age and he isn't married yet; here he is wasting his sweetness on the desert air in Gartmore. Do you think you could use your influence to find him a wife?'

'A marriage bureau in the Áras. Now that's a good idea,' she quipped.

At the end of the meal the President diplomatically declined Father Ryan's invitation to adjourn to the sitting-room for a drink and went instead to the kitchen to thank the ladies. She said her good-byes and waved as her car drove away. There was a great feeling of satisfaction that the whole thing had gone well. As they all went back into the house to finish out the night Paddy turned to Father Ryan: 'Be the jizzes Father, it won't change our livin' or our dyin', but Gartmore is no longer in the back of beyond.'

The Dinner Party

Kay was glad the dinner party was in her house. She and Edward would not have to go out into a cold, wet February evening and return in similar discomfort in the small hours of the morning. They could shower and dress in their warm bedroom, descend their elegant stairs, put the finishing touches to the table and in the comfort of their beautifully proportioned drawing-room await the arrival of their guests. They had not had a dinner party for some time. Kay felt that their turn was overdue and Edward was keen to invite some of his business contacts.

Kay was a graduate in English literature and Edward a graduate in law. They met at university but neither had the slightest interest in the discipline of the other. Their marriage had held together fairly well because early on they began to live in separate worlds that did not often intersect. Whereas Kay's interest was one she pursued for pleasure, Edward pursued his, not for love of the law, but simply to make money and execute as many 'strokes' as possible. Kay, a full-time housewife and a voracious reader, made no attempt to discuss books she was reading with Edward. She pursued her interest with a small reading circle and always looked forward eagerly to the evenings when the group was due to meet. Edward seldom mentioned his work. Kay was delighted that their two boys were reading for arts degrees; one English literature and the other French and Italian.

Edward was a senior partner in one of the city's top solicitor practices. He seemed to Kay to achieve great satisfaction from dealing with the big businessmen amongst his clients. He knew many of the people whose names appeared from time to time in the business pages of the newspaper and some whose speculative commercial enterprises during the boom had, since the recession, made them household names. He invited some of these people with their wives to dinner parties. Tonight was one such occasion when two couples were Edward's business contacts and one couple were friends of Kay.

Edward was from a family of accountants, father and brother, both of whom, when he chose law considered it a betrayal. He was tall, slender, wore rimless glasses and kept his thinning dark hair sleeked back on his head like a head waiter in an expensive restaurant. Apart from gardening and holidays he wore a suit with waistcoat and even to his legal partners he looked distinctly old-fashioned.

The doorbell rang. Edward answered. It was Evelyn and David. They stood under a large umbrella they had used walking the few yards from the car.

'What a night,' said Edward, 'come in, come in.'

'Will it ever stop raining?' David said, 'the only thing that could make me go back to America is the Irish weather.' He let down the umbrella and Edward took it and their coats, put them on the large carved wood hallstand and ushered them into the drawing-room.

'We're first again,' said Evelyn, 'this husband of mine is a stickler for time. Even though I delayed as best I could we're still first.'

'That's fine,' said Kay, embracing Evelyn and offering her cheek to David.

Evelyn had been in the same year in college as Kay, and David had come to Ireland on a teacher exchange and had stayed. They both taught in one of the city's prestigious boarding-schools and Evelyn was in the reading circle with Kay. They sat down. Edward stayed standing and asked:

'What can I get you to drink?' The doorbell rang. 'I'll get them all together.'

When Edward came back he preceded Jack and Fiona into the room. Kay stood up, greeted the new arrivals and introduced them to Evelyn and David. The women talked together, and after Edward had poured the drinks he and Jack spoke together and David, sitting close to the flaming log fire heard snippets of their conversation:

'……but there was no word before I left the office.'

'If you don't hear first thing on Monday ring him, he's a blackguard.'

David looked towards the women who were deep in conversation.

The doorbell rang again. Edward left the room. Jack straightened his bright red tie and adjusted the matching handkerchief in his top pocket. He had started life as a carpenter in the West of Ireland. When he came to Dublin in his early twenties to do house repairs and extensions he watched carefully, and learned quickly to imitate the professional people he met, in dress and social habits. He looked around the room at the pictures and then realising that David was sitting nearby on his own he asked:

'And what do you do?'

'I'm a schoolmaster.'

'A man in a boy's world and a boy in a man's world, eh?'

David bit his tongue. He noticed the fine material of Jack's suit and felt distinctly scruffy in his sports jacket and cords. He had only one suit and that came out once a year, along with his academic hood, on school prize-giving day.

'And what do you do?'

'I develop properties.' David was glad he had held his fire.

'You mean you're a developer. That doesn't make a boy in a man's world sound so bad.'

Just then Edward came in with Pat and Trish, introduced them to Evelyn and David and asked what they would have to drink. David thought he knew Pat's face from somewhere. Searching around in his head, and not listening to the conversation, he tumbled to it; his photo was on the cover of a book he had read recently about the building bubble and the bank collapse. He was a senior banker, but in appearance, including his well-cut tweed suit, he looked more like a gentleman farmer. He had joined the bank from school and worked his way up. He was proud of that and believed that he was entitled to the bounty that the building boom had brought him. 'I put in the hard slog over the years and I deserve it,' he used to say to his wife, but she hadn't heard him say that recently.

'Will we go in?' Kay said and pulled the guard across in front of the fire. She led the way into the large dining-room with the elaborately set table. Jack surveyed the pictures and took in the table setting. Kay seated the party. David turned to Trish on his left and made a comment on the weather.

*

It was still raining heavily when Jack drove down the avenue just before 1.30 am.

'My God, that's a turn up for the books,' Fiona said quietly and sat back into the passenger seat.

'I can't believe it,' said Jack, and fell silent. After a minute or so Fiona said:

'A penny for your thoughts.'

'I'm just thinking.'

'What are you thinking?'

'I was just thinking about that bollocks of an American.'

'That's not what I meant.'

'I know it's not, but that's what I was thinking.'

'I mean about Edward.'

'There's been some mistake,' and Jack fell silent again.

'Anyway, what was wrong with the American?'

'He said that all the developers that owed millions and the bankers that lent it to them should end up in prison and the Government should be exposed for their corruption in enabling them. Not a word about the prosperity they created for everybody;

wonderful infrastructure, full employment, fine social welfare benefits. People were never so well off.'

'But look at the country now. You know as well as I do that between the lot of you, you destroyed the economy for generations to come, all for pure greed and to satisfy inflated egos.'

'Shut up. I told you never to talk to me like that again, and anyway nothing of that has anything to do with Edward.'

'Has it not? How do you know?'

'He isn't a developer or a banker or even a politician.'

'No, but he provided a service that enabled the madness. It looks as if, to say the least, he bent the rules. I hope the Guards aren't waiting for us when we get home.' Jack fumed, but said nothing. There was another long silence.

'David's a schoolteacher,' said Fiona.

'I know he's a bloody schoolteacher. He teaches English and do you know what his great love is? Poetry. We'd be waiting a long time for him and his likes to improve people's standard of living. Poetry, Holy God. Poetry. The sissy.'

'I haven't heard your mantra for a long time: "I left school at fourteen and look where I am now." Look where you are now is right: owing the banks millions. Bloody marvellous.' Jack slammed on the brakes. Her safety belt saved Fiona from hitting the windscreen. The rain drummed on the roof of the car while the wipers struggled to keep the windscreen clear.

'Get out of the fucking car.'

'No.'

'If you don't shut up I'll put you out.'

Not another word passed between them until they arrived home. Jack spent the best part of an hour on the telephone and by the time he arrived upstairs Fiona was asleep.

Pat and Trish left shortly after Jack and Fiona. Pat asked Trish to drive.

'Have you had too much to drink?'

'Probably, but I'm stunned about Edward, even if he is only helping with enquiries.'

'He's not just helping with enquiries, he's been arrested. He's going to be charged with something. He'll be held in custody over the weekend until a judge grants him bail.'

'How do you know?'

'Kay told me. When she went outside she spoke to the Guards.'

'Dear God. Are you sure?'

'That's what Kay told me.'

Neither of them spoke for the next few minutes. Then Pat said:

'Do you know what that bloody schoolteacher said?'

'About Edward?'

'No, about the economic crash. The man's a simpleton. He said that he couldn't understand how we didn't see it coming. That even first-formers could tell you that bubbles burst, what goes up must come down and tigers die.'

'That's far too simple for bankers to understand,' said Fiona. There was another silence.

'I tried to explain to him that if the regulator had done his job we wouldn't be in this mess. We did what all good footballers do. We played the whistle.'

'The trouble is what you were doing wasn't football.'

'He said we should pay back our bonuses.'

'There's a certain logic to that. You drummed up business in cahoots with the developers and took bonuses on notional figures. Then you're surprised when the whole thing collapsed like a pack of cards.'

When Pat and Trish arrived home the phone was ringing. Pat answered it in the hall and Trish went upstairs to bed. When Pat arrived into the bedroom he recounted the conversation.

'That was Kay. She's been on to one of Edward's partners. He says they'll want an independent surety for bail and she wants me to provide it.'

'And will you?'

'I will, if I can find an insurance company that will give me a bond.'

Evelyn and David were last to leave. Kay had signalled to Evelyn to stay behind and confessed that she hadn't the remotest idea what it was all about. She was composed and her only concern was to contact the boys both of whom were out for the night and neither was answering his mobile.

As David drove down the avenue he said:

'I'm not surprised when he's in league with those two.'

'Why what's wrong with them?'

'They're mindless. They do what they do for no other reason than that they can. Neither of them has even one brain cell that says "think for yourself."'

As they drove, their concern was for Kay and the boys. The rain had passed by the time they arrived home. They stood out of the car and looked up in awe at the crystal clear moonlit sky. They picked out a few constellations and then stood for a few moments in silence. They took some deep breaths of clear night air and went inside.

Internal Audit

Frank had just had the call he had been dreading. He put down the phone and stared straight at the open file on his desk without seeing a thing. He felt trapped in his musty cream-coloured office with high ceiling and damaged cornice that had once been the gracious room of a Georgian townhouse. There were files on the floor and anywhere else there was space; there was shabbiness everywhere, and Frank's head was somewhere else. The internal auditors would be starting in his section on Monday morning.

Frank had joined the Civil Service straight from school. He had married Moira when they were both in their mid-twenties and they had two daughters. The two girls were married and gone, and about a year ago Moira developed cancer. She had had a terrible time, and their health insurance was hopelessly inadequate to provide the private treatment she needed. Frank was at his wit's end to give her not only the best treatment available, but when the worst became inevitable he was determined that at any cost she should have private nursing-care to the end. All of this was away beyond his insurance cover and his salary, so Frank had exploited a flaw in the system that he had become aware of some time after he was posted to Finance.

The internal auditors, for obvious reasons, didn't signal ahead their intention to work in a particular section. Frank, through a contact, without giving rise to suspicion, was able to know where they were going next. He had been quite confident all along that his embezzlement would not be discovered, but now that the time approached for the audit he began to have niggling doubts.

He could forget the matter for periods of the day during work, but at lunchtime and after he left the office he became preoccupied with the audit and how thorough it would be. After work, even when Moira was still alive, he used to go for a pint and a chaser to a pub on his way home. On the nights since he had word of the audit he would stand at the bar going over and over the likely questions the auditors would ask, and rehearsed the answers in his head. So much so that the barman and other regulars became aware that he was preoccupied and put it down to his recent bereavement.

At night Frank would fall asleep for a couple of hours, waken and then lie awake till morning. He was obsessed with the embezzlement and the audit, convinced in the middle of the night that he would be found out. He went over in his mind the consequences of this: the sack, the loss of pension and above all, the shame. How would he ever face his two girls again, their husbands and his grandson. He would explain that he didn't do it for drink, horses or exotic holidays, but for Moira, and he convinced himself that they would understand or even admire him for it. He wished he could turn back the clock and tried to work out where he could find the significant sum of money he needed to refund it. He knew that even if he could come up with the money, he wouldn't be able to return it unknown to the auditors. He thought if he could volunteer it immediately, he might forestall his sacking and simply be demoted. This way he would at least avoid the shame as nobody outside would need to know.

When morning came his spirits would lift. He would convince himself that the loophole in the system, which he had been aware of over the years and had finally exploited, would not betray him, but he feared that the computerised system might throw up something that he couldn't take account of. On balance, however, on the bus to work he was confident, but during the rest of the day he oscillated between confidence and composing what he would say to the girls and to a judge in court.

By the Friday Frank had reduced the whole thing to the need to tell one lie to avoid being found out, and this would not be difficult for him, since he had told many the lie over the years to hide another secret.

When he was a boy he was always interested in his sister's clothes – the items he liked and didn't like. He noticed things that went well together or didn't match. He even noticed his mother's clothes. Once when everybody was out he put on a blouse and skirt of his sister and admired himself in the mirror. In adolescence he went through dreadful contortions that he might be homosexual, but he emerged into adulthood a full-blooded heterosexual male.

After he became secure in his heterosexuality he was more at ease with himself and his aberration and remembers well the day in his late teens that he read an article in a magazine that put a name on his interest in women's clothes. In fact when he read this article it was the first time he admitted to himself that he was interested in wearing them. The article said that the whole business was harmless

138

and resulted from some minor glitch in early development, and the only difficulty was the response of people who didn't understand. It made the point that after the transvestite dressed he felt a peace that relieved an incipient tension that had built up inside him. The danger was, however, that cross-dressing might become an obsession and like any obsession it could become unhealthy.

Frank was relieved that he wasn't some kind of freak, and when he was alone in the house he would dress in some of his sister's clothes. In fact he engineered opportunities to be alone, and he did develop an obsession; an obsession that nobody on earth would ever find out.

In his early twenties he had had a series of girlfriends and occasionally wondered when he was out with one of them: 'What would she think if she knew?' He also wondered from time to time what the lads he played football with would think. If either of them had to know he would prefer that it was the girls, for he was sure that they would be more understanding than the lads, who would ridicule him beyond endurance. In banter they ridiculed anything that was a chink in the armour of the all-conquering macho heterosexual male.

Then he met Moira and he was bowled over. He knew early on that this was the woman for him, and he was blissfully happy when he discovered that he was the one for her. His interest in dressing diminished and for periods disappeared altogether. He did, however, wonder from time to time how she would take it if she knew, but he was determined that she would never know. For a while he even felt it might have been a phase he had gone through that had disappeared, now that he had met the love of his life. It wasn't; it was still there.

Frank and Moira married and in due course the girls arrived, grew up and flew the nest. Moira was a full-time wife and mother, and Frank moved slowly up the ladder in the Civil Service. He kept his secret under wraps, filling his need to dress only under the safest conditions, that is until Moira died. Since he was now in the house alone he indulged himself more freely and more often. He would spend an evening trying on Moira's dresses, most of which, if he were to look well in them, he would have to have altered. He even began to plan how he might do this. He began to dress fully, wearing jewellery and make-up. Then one night after dark when he had spent a long session dressing, wearing a wig that Moira had had when she was having chemotherapy, he went out to the car and drove into town. At traffic-lights he kept his hands at the bottom of the steering wheel, because of all his visible parts he felt his hands were most likely to give him away. When he arrived into the city centre he parked the car and sat for a while, then did a circuit and drove home again. He felt a certain freedom and was satisfied that nobody had looked strangely at him.

He did this a number of nights before he had the courage to park the car and walk thirty or forty yards to a shop, buy an evening paper and back to the car. When he did it nobody blinked, and he was elated. During the working day he took to going to work, dressed in Moira's underwear, and over it his conventional grey suit, collar and tie and black shoes. He started doing this occasionally, but soon he did it every day.

The Monday morning arrived that his departmental internal audit was due. Frank had more or less convinced himself that his embezzlement would not be detected. He worked away awaiting the arrival of the auditors, but he could not apply himself properly to anything. He made numerous cups of coffee and by lunchtime the auditors had not arrived. After lunch he worked himself into a panic. He almost felt he would prefer if they walked in the door and told him they knew exactly what he had done; it would be over and he would handle whatever he had to face. Not knowing was infinitely worse than being found out.

That night Frank slept badly. He was torn between how well he felt recently about dressing and how badly he felt about the prospect of the exposure of his embezzlement. If only he had the audit successfully out of the way he could relax and have the prospect of something of a satisfying life. He was lonely and missed Moira, but he felt, not without some guilt, the benefit of being free of her distressing final illness. He also felt some ambivalence about wearing her clothes, but this ambivalence was diminishing with time.

On Tuesday morning when he arrived into the office he tried to do some work but couldn't concentrate. He bit the head off a junior who came into his room with a query. By lunchtime, when there was no sign of the auditors, Frank was pacing around the room like a caged lion. His stomach alternated between being in a knot and feeling sick. His hands were shaking and he had a dreadful headache. Instead of his usual sandwich and apple for lunch he went down to the pub and had three quick brandies. Back at work he felt worse. He reported sick and left the office, risking not being there to deceive the auditors if they came during the afternoon.

On the way home he called to his local. Standing at the bar, waiting to be served, he had a session of trying to burp, then he put his two hands to his chest and bent double in pain. He collapsed, and as he lay on the floor someone opened his tie and his belt. Still conscious he fumbled to keep his belt closed. When the ambulance arrived he was unconscious. By the time they were at the hospital it was too late.

When one of his daughters arrived at the hospital she was brought immediately to identify Frank's body and she brought home in a plastic bag his spectacles, his watch, his wallet and his clothes.

Home Again

Rita shook Fred to waken him from his evening sleep beside the fire.

'There's an old woman at the door who says she's Auntie Kay from Canada. She has the wrong farm. You'd better talk to her, maybe you'd know who she's looking for. It must be Whelans.'

Rita handed Fred the receiver. 'You phone them.'

Fred began to dial and stopped short.

'It couldn't be! My father once told me of a sister of his that went to Canada who was in touch a few times and they never heard from her again. He said she was probably long since dead.'

Rita had answered a ring at the back door. It was dusk and she was just in time to see the lights of a taxi leave through the yard gate. Standing there beside a large suitcase was a woman that she judged to be in her eighties. Medium height and stooped, she was well-dressed but somewhat dishevelled.

'I've come home,' she said. Rita looked at her blankly. 'I'm Auntie Kay.' Rita wondered which of the neighbours she was looking for.

'You have the wrong house.'

'No I haven't. This is it; it's changed, but this is it. I was born in this house. I left for Canada over sixty years ago.'

It was starting to rain.

'Will you stand into the porch and wait a moment please. I'll tell my husband.'

Rita pushed back boots and wellingtons with her foot to make room and dragged the old lady's case into the porch. 'I won't be a minute.'

Fred went down to the kitchen and found the old woman sitting at the table.

'You must be Ned's son, you have a great look of him.' Fred pulled out a chair and sat down.

'My father was Edward Staunton, who are you?'

'I'm his sister Kathleen. I've come home to die.'

It didn't take Fred long to confirm the old woman's identity, and when he was in no doubt that she was his aunt, he called Rita from the sitting-room.

'Rita, come and meet my Auntie Kathleen.' Rita covered her surprise with a smile, feeling guilty that she had left the old woman standing in the porch. She shook her hand and said:

'I'm delighted to meet you. Sixty years is a long time.'

After they had finally settled Auntie Kay into the spare bedroom, they went to their own room and before they went to sleep, they had covered a hundred questions about her; past, present and future.

Next morning Rita brought up a cup of tea to Auntie Kay. In bed the old woman looked even smaller and older than she had done the night before.

'I hope you slept well; you were tired after your journey. Stay there and I'll bring up your breakfast.'

'I can't stand breakfast in bed.'

Fred had milked, he'd been back for his breakfast and gone again, the children had gone to school and there was still no sign of Auntie Kay. At about ten o'clock she arrived down to the kitchen. Rita enquired:

'What would you like?'

'I never have more than coffee and a bagel.'

'We have no bagels, but I'll make toast.'

Rita didn't like to ask too many questions but on every topic that came up Auntie Kay soon declaimed with great authority, closing down any hope of real conversation.

'Would you like to come to the village with me, I need a few messages?'

'Yes, I'll come to the village.'

In the shops Auntie Kay would ask the name of whoever was behind the counter and tell them that they must be related to so-and-so long since dead, or inform them that their families weren't from around here. On the way home she went on about how everything had changed so much and showed surprise at every manifestation of modernity.

At dinner, midday, she made it plain that she was used to only a snack at this time of day and in Canada she had dinner in the evening. Fred, though circumspect, was less reluctant than Rita to ask Auntie Kay questions. He elicited little hard information about either her past or her plans. The little bit of information she did give was riddled with inconsistencies so that Fred and Rita were unsure if she was laundering the truth, but they suspected that at least part of it was caused by her age. The only piece of unequivocal information she did give reiterated what she had said the night she arrived:

'I've come home to die.'

When the two girls came in from school, they were excited to meet their great-aunt from Canada. She looked at them in a detached sort of way and said:

'Since you have no brother to take over the farm, one of you will have to marry a farmer.' She took out her purse and gave each of them some Canadian coins.

As the days passed Fred and Rita were able to piece together a little about Auntie Kay. She had worked all her life in the same office. She had never been married and was heavily involved in her local parish. She had lived in an apartment that she had left in the hands of an estate agent to be sold, and she wanted to be buried with her own people.

After a while there was no mention of Auntie Kay's plans. Fred and Rita speculated that when she sold her flat she would buy something locally, however they were afraid that she couldn't survive living on her own; she never offered to help in the kitchen, she was forgetful and worst of all Rita had had to put a plastic under-sheet on her bed.

One evening in the sitting-room, after the girls had gone to bed, Fred took the bull by the horns:

'Auntie Kay, where do you hope to find accommodation? You'll have to go to the town to find something to suit you.'

'I'm fine where I am. This is my home and the room is comfortable.'

If the old woman had had a sense of humour Fred and Rita would have thought she was joking, but it was obvious that she was not. They were stunned into silence. They looked at each other and Rita who had taken the brunt of her intrusion mouthed to Fred: 'Go on.' Fred needed no encouragement.

'You can't stay here; we have the girls to rear and a farm to run.'

'This is my home; I was born in this house. I know it's a long time but I've returned at last.'

Not another word was spoken. When they were in their bedroom, Rita and Fred still couldn't quite take it in.

Next day Fred went to see the parish priest who was able to find for him the name and telephone number of Auntie Kay's parish in Canada. That evening Fred phoned.

'Father Ford?'

'Yes.' Fred explained who he was.

'I hope she arrived safely. We miss her in the parish.'

'Would you be kind enough to contact the estate agent and tell him to take her apartment off the market and I'll phone you again?'

'I will; has she changed her mind? She always talked so warmly about her old home; in fact I could describe it to you she told me about it so often, and she was determined to spend her last days there, bless her.'

'Thank you for your help, Father. I'll phone you again in a few days.'

Things didn't improve but Fred and Rita wanted to leave time for 'you can't stay here' to sink in. They lost no opportunity to make reference from time to time to the implications of it, but the old woman behaved as though Fred had never said it. One evening in the sitting-room Fred broached the subject again.

'Auntie Kay, you remember I told you it wasn't possible for you to stay here, well we'll help you to find something suitable in town.'

'I'm not living in any town. I was born and brought up in the country that's where I want to end my days. I lived in the city long enough.'

'You won't find suitable accommodation in the country, what about the village?'

'The village is somewhere you go to shop and come home again. I'm fine where I am.'

Fred and Rita thought as much; she had refused to listen, but they had wanted to give her every opportunity to make some alternative arrangement. There was nothing else for it now but to put their contingency plan into operation. Rita went to the travel agent in town the following morning and booked a flight to Toronto a week hence. That evening when they were together Fred told Auntie Kay what they had done. There was no response.

'Did you hear me Auntie Kay? Your flight is 4.30 pm next Wednesday. We'll drive you to the airport and I've spoken to Father Ford. He'll meet you off the plane in Toronto.'

'By the way,' the old woman said, 'did I tell you about your brother? The one your father had with Mary Cleary of the cottage that I brought to Canada as a baby and reared as my own son.'

Fred was astounded, but he was immediately suspicious that she had brought this up in this circumstance.

'No you didn't,' he said, 'and I don't want to know.' Nothing was going to stop them putting her on the plane.

A few days later when she didn't appear for breakfast, Rita went up to her room.

'I'm not well,' she said, 'I had a bad night.' Rita ignored the comment as the childish strategy she knew it to be and helped her to dress.

In the kitchen the following day Rita said to the old woman:

'I'll help you to pack tomorrow. I have your clean laundry ready.'

During the day Auntie Kay was quieter than usual, but she made no reference to her departure for Toronto and she made no further reference to a brother of Fred. That evening she only picked at her food and she sat on in the sitting-room longer than usual. When she eventually went to bed Fred said to Rita:

'She's hoping we'll feel sorry for her. It's clear she's used to having her own way. I've arranged for Paddy to do the evening milking on Wednesday so we can both go to the airport. I wouldn't put it past her to employ some other last-ditch tactic in order not to go. We won't know ourselves when things are back to normal, and the children certainly won't miss her.'

When Auntie Kay was not down again at her usual time for breakfast in the morning, Rita went upstairs. She knocked on her door. There was no reply.

'The old soldier again,' Rita thought to herself. She knocked again. There was no response. She turned the handle, pushed open

149

the door slowly and saw the old woman on the floor beside the bed. Rita called her name: 'Auntie Kay, Auntie Kay.' She shook her, but she didn't move. She took her wrist. It was cold and there was no pulse.

As Rita arrived down to the kitchen the phone rang.

A man's voice with a Canadian accent said:

'Hello, I've been talking to Father Ford. Can I speak to my mother please? I want to tell her that her apartment's been sold and she can't come back to Toronto.'

Friends

The most unlikely association of any two people in the district was between Paddy and Richard. Neither of them came from the village, and since they were both blow-ins the indigenous population felt no responsibility for either of them. Each was the antithesis of the other; Paddy spent every waking moment making or planning to make money, while Richard had no more interest in money than the man in the moon. The locals may not have felt any responsibility for them, but that didn't mean they were ignored. On the contrary, they were both the subject of constant gossip, for each was guilty of one of the two unforgivable sins of rural Ireland: Paddy was a financial success, and Richard had no religion whatever; he wasn't even a Protestant.

Paddy, in his late forties, was small, of average build with a head of dark-brown hair. When he met you his round face rippled into a charming smile, accompanied by an earnest enquiry for the health and wellbeing of yourself and all belonging to you. Beneath this natural and winning charm was an acute intelligence that had a firm grasp of how business worked, and a determination to make it work for him. He was less of an outsider than Richard, in that he was from the county, but when he came to live in the village he was a stranger. He came as a youth straight from school to work on the building of the first County Council estate, and when it was finished he stayed on and worked as a labourer in the area for a few years before going to Dublin. He reappeared in the village eight years later, set himself up as a builder and never looked back.

As far as Richard was concerned, nobody knew of any connection that he might have with the district. Recently he had bought a cottage up a long lane, a mile outside the village. His arrival was the cause of much speculation: he was variously believed to be the last survivor of the great train robbers, an unfrocked priest and a communist spy. Whereas Paddy was married with a family, Richard lived alone, but one rumour had it that he had a wife and children in England.

In due course it emerged that he was a university lecturer who had taken early retirement and wanted to live in the country. He was tall, thin and angular and bald with a few wisps on top. He lived to himself, appearing in the village once or twice a week for provisions. He was polite but formal and didn't fit into any sector of the local community.

One day Paddy was walking land adjoining Richard's cottage with a local auctioneer, with a view to buying another stretch of the only commodity that could establish beyond doubt that he was a man of substance. This was not land upon which to build, but to invest in and to farm. He was passing close to the ditch when Richard came out to throw scraps to his hens.

'Good morning.'

Paddy knew as little about Richard as anyone did and was glad of the opportunity to talk to him.

'They're not economical, but it's great to have the fresh eggs,' said Paddy.

'These ones are still in credit but I'm more interested in the quality of the eggs than the economics.'

By this time Paddy was on the ditch at the end of the garden.

'There's nothing like living in the country.'

'No matter where you live there are pros and cons; on balance I prefer the country.'

'You need a lot of money to live well in the city.'

Richard did not respond. Paddy went on:

'I suppose it depends on what you want.'

Richard finished scattering the scraps, turned up the saucepan and tapped the bottom.

'True.'

He turned towards the cottage and Paddy re-joined the auctioneer.

In due course Paddy bought the land and as with the other pieces of land he had acquired, he stocked it with the help of a rogue of a cattle dealer for whom he had once built a house. He used to admit freely when he first bought cattle that if a beast were sick it would have to come up and tell him. However, he learned quickly and developed a good eye, and now did the herding himself, which brought him into contact with Richard from time to time.

At first they talked over the ditch; Richard was cautious of Paddy's charming smile and his questions. Paddy's curiosity, however, was not of the idle kind but arose from a genuine surprise that a man like Richard, who had in abundance the one thing he didn't have himself – education, should throw everything up and come to live in a cottage up a lane at the back end of nowhere. Richard in turn found Paddy perceptive and intelligent and eventually invited him into the cottage.

'Coffee?'

'No thanks.'

'Well I'm having one. Tea?'

'Thanks.'

Richard went out to the kitchen at the back. Paddy looked around the room. Most of the downstairs of the original cottage had been made into a single room with a wood burning stove at one end. It was untidy but comfortable; there were mats of various kinds on the original floor of stone flags. There was a substantial leather upholstered armchair facing the stove, with a small table beside it on which was an angle-poise lamp, a tobacco pouch, two pipes and all the paraphernalia and grime that go with smoking a pipe. Under the front window was a refectory-type oak table, covered almost entirely with books apart from a small area at the end near the stove. On this there was a used cereal bowl and spoon, a milk jug, a plate and knife, a napkin in a ring, a pot of marmalade and a set of condiments. Opposite was a glass-fronted bookcase, full of books, and more books in piles on every available surface and on the floor. There were pictures positioned randomly on the walls, and at the opposite end to the stove there was a large piece of abstract sculpture in wood that was out of proportion to everything else in the room.

Richard reappeared, riddled the stove, opened it and threw in a couple of logs.

'Sit down.'

The only chairs that hadn't books on them were the leather armchair and one at the dining end of the table. Paddy spotted a stool under the table that he pulled out and sat on. Richard closed the door of the stove, increased the draught and went back to the kitchen. For a moment Paddy thought of the building site and wondered if the roof trusses had been delivered, but it didn't seem to matter; it was all aeons away; he was in another world.

Richard came back, made space and put a tray on the table.

'I suppose you'll soon have to make up your mind whether you're a builder or a farmer.'

'I don't think so. When it's a matter of either/or I usually take both.'

'Will you have time for both?'

'What I haven't time for I can pay someone to do. Anyway the brother runs the building for me; leaves me time to think and plan. You have to think and plan if you want to stay ahead.'

'Stay ahead of whom?'

'Everybody else. There's only a certain amount of money out there and it's a case of getting what you can before someone else does.'

Richard opened the stove door and sat back into his chair.

'What do you want all this money for?'

'It's the way people give you respect; they think more of you in a brand new Merc than a third-hand "banger". Anyway it's a challenge. I like being a step ahead.'

'Where does that leave me with no car at all?'

'That's different.'

'Why?'

'You have something else.'

'What do you mean?'

'You have education.'

'Would the people who envy your Merc think as much of my education?'

'They wouldn't, but I would, and what I'd really like is both, but it's too late now.'

Paddy, still in his overcoat, moved back from the stove which gave out great heat. Between the stove and the tea Paddy was too hot. He put down his mug and undid the buttons of his overcoat.

'Take it off.'

'Ah, I better be going.'

He opened his coat and picked up his mug.

'Have you read all these books?'

'Most of them, at some stage.'

'Why do you keep them?'

'I sometimes wonder, especially since I moved here, but there's something about books that makes it hard to part with them.'

There followed a long silence and then Paddy spoke:

'Much and all as I need education I'm not sure what it is.'

'It's knowing enough to know what you don't know. To say you're not sure what it is, is a good start.'

There was a further silence while Paddy tried to make sense of this, then Richard went on:

'It's part of what marks us off from the animals – our ability to reflect on our condition, to make ourselves the object of our own thought, and speculate about why we're here and what we're doing. Despite having that capacity, most people don't use it. They take everything on trust from other people who have the arrogance to think they have all the answers.'

'Do you mean the Church?'

'The Church, the State, big business. All the institutions.'

Paddy stood up and this time he took his coat off and pushed his stool a little further away from the fire.

'I go to mass every Sunday and perform all my religious duties, and believe that if I didn't I wouldn't thrive.'

'Getting on is nothing to do with religion, Paddy. That's superstition, pure superstition. Religion has to do with trying to make sense of this mysterious life we have to live. It's nothing to do with making money or believing there's a God who'll look after you if you behave yourself.'

Paddy noticed that for the first time Richard had used his name; it somehow helped to build a trust between the uneducated builder-cum-farmer and the retired academic.

Paddy knew he had to go. If the trusses hadn't been delivered the men would be wasting time. He stood up and put on his coat, and Richard went with him as far as the back door. Paddy went

157

down the garden and over the ditch. A delicate covering of frosted cobwebs lay like a mantle of lace on the gorse and along the ditches. The sun had made no impression on the blanket of grey mist. Paddy buttoned his coat against the cold that he felt intensely after the warmth of the room. He reached his car and drove back to the village. He arrived at the site and found that everything was in order. His interlude in the cottage was still buzzing in his head.

Once or twice during the day he remembered his early morning cup of tea and the warm comfortable room full of books. There were many questions he had, but felt he couldn't ask on his first visit. What did Richard do all day? What was the big piece of sculpture? Then there was the one he couldn't ask: had he money?

That evening, although it was unusual for him to talk to Teresa about his day, when he arrived home he stood in the kitchen and told her everything about Richard and the cottage. He went into the sitting-room to watch the news but couldn't concentrate. He looked around the large room with expensive furniture and an expanse of flower-patterned carpet, the luxurious suite with elaborate trim, the ceiling to floor velvet curtains and escalloped pelmets with swags and tassels. There were cheap reproduction pictures on the walls and a gilt standard lamp beside the television. There wasn't one book in the room. Apart from the youngsters' schoolbooks there probably wasn't one book in the house.

After tea Paddy talked to Teresa again about Richard.

'What's the use of an education like he has if you don't use it to make something of yourself?'

'He has made something of himself.'

'But he doesn't contribute to the economy, or give employment. If we all sat around reading books all day the country'd be in a queer state.'

Richard was in the garden the next time Paddy was herding. He asked him in again. This time Paddy wasn't so awe-struck.

'Do you mind me asking you a question?'

Richard pulled out a chair for him.

'You can ask me anything you like.'

Paddy sat down.

'What do you do all day?'

'I have breakfast, clean the fire, wash dishes, then I read and write a bit. Some days I do some washing or go to the village for groceries or perhaps for a walk. Then I may read again, and I have to cook. There isn't much spare time.'

'What do you write?'

'Letters. I keep in touch with my friends, and other bits and pieces.'

Richard went into the kitchen and reappeared with a mug of tea and a mug of coffee. He gave the tea to Paddy and sat down.

'And do you not feel the need to achieve something?'

'I achieve a lot. I survive and I have time to myself to read.'

'Yes, but if you don't do something practical or produce something what do you have from life? To have satisfaction you need competition; to best somebody.'

Richard pared some tobacco and packed it into his pipe.

'That's a bottomless pit, Paddy. I did it for long enough. The more you're ahead the more you need to go further and the deeper you dig yourself into the pit, and the reason you do it is to have the approval of other people, and at the end of the day nobody else gives a damn about you.'

Richard lit his pipe while Paddy assimilated what he had said. He flicked his match onto the hearth and went on:

'Your need for other people's approval means you're letting them run your life, and I was fed up with other people running my life.'

That gave Paddy a handle on the conversation that he grabbed hold of and took off in his own direction, missing the point:

'Nobody else runs my life, and the more money I have the freer I am of other people.'

'You may be free in small things, but the more money you have the more you want and the more precarious you become as you risk more to accumulate more. You become enslaved to your own ego and become more dependent on people who work for you and the bank manager who lends you money.' This was more in Paddy's line than talk of digging the kind of pits Richard talked about.

'I'm not depending on them, they depend on me and if I win they win and if I lose, which I have no intention of doing, they lose, and that's what makes life interesting. If there was no risk there would be no kick in winning.'

Soon Paddy didn't need to be invited into the cottage, but called from time to time when he was herding. After he sold the cattle, on a day he was passing on the way back to the village he would drive up the long lane to Richard's cottage and the two would sit and talk for ages. Richard sometimes went with Paddy on his trips to Dublin and inevitably had a bag of books with him on the way home.

Paddy would banter:

'Haven't you enough of those auld books without buying more? It'd suit you better to put a lick of paint on that cottage of yours.'

'Paint on the windows won't improve my quality of life. Anyway if I do that I'll only have to do it again in a few years.'

'No matter what, I still envy you your education.'

'All anyone needs in order to be better educated is to make up their mind to it, and to a man of your intelligence and determination that should be no trouble.'

'I've left it too late.'

'It's never too late. The problem is "the master" won't let you.'

'You'd be in a quare way without "the master" all the same, and anyway money is not my master, it's what it can do for you.'

One morning Paddy called to the cottage to return a book that Richard had insisted he ought to read. He sat to the stove while Richard made the tea.

'Thanks for the book.'

'Well what did you think of it?'

'Richard, there's something I have to tell you, that in the whole world only my wife knows.' He hesitated, and Richard waited. Looking into the stove Paddy said: 'I'm not able to read or write. I'm illiterate.'

There was a pause while Richard took it in, and to mitigate Paddy's obvious embarrassment he said:

'Well I can't imagine what you'd have achieved if you could.'

This embarrassing revelation made no difference to their friendship that continued as before. In fact it heightened Richard's admiration for Paddy, an admiration that was tinged with sadness at what in other circumstances might have been.

Assignations

'I can't do this much longer' Kay thought to herself as she stood up from the flowerbed and stretched. She supported her lower back on both sides with her hands to relieve the stiffness that was verging on pain. Gardening was her great love, but she was finding it physically more and more difficult. She had been widowed for five years and lived alone and so far she had succeeded in maintaining the large garden of the house in which she had lived all her married life.

Still holding one side of her back she put her gardening gloves and tools into the potting-shed where for some reason the musty smell always brought her back to the early days when she was married, into which she dipped in memory from time to time to remind herself of how lucky she had been. It was autumn and the heat had gone out of the day. She would light the fire as she did every evening through the winter. She looked forward to the long evenings when she brought her dinner to the sitting-room on a tray and sat beside the fire to read. Recently, however, despite her well-being and her comforts, she had become more and more conscious that there was something missing in her life.

Kay had discovered from experience what she had heard widows say over the years; after the death of her husband she was invited less and less to the homes of their friends and in fact some of them had dropped her altogether. She had a good relationship with her sister Marjorie who lived a little distance away and was also a widow. Kay had always enjoyed the company of men, not in any romantic or flirtatious way, but she found their conversation, when it wasn't golf, more interesting than that of women. She was constantly aware of one of the many wise things she had learned from Jim, her husband, that you cannot sit around and hope that circumstances or other people will make things happen for you. If you want something enough you must make it happen.

In recent years in her gardening magazine she had seen columns of advertisements placed by people seeking introductions to members of the opposite sex. Naturally when Jim was alive she paid them scant attention and she never, in her wildest dreams, thought she might use them. During the past year, however, she wondered from time to time whether she might. These were not the kind of ads she had seen in a tabloid paper a workman had left behind in the house. This was a highly respected magazine read by serious gardeners and most of the ads sought companionship and to share an interest in gardening.

Kay was clear in her mind that there must be men out there who had been widowed and who would be good company, have a value system similar to her own and of course share a love of gardening. She would enjoy the company of a man with his own house, a couple of times a week. She would have an escort with whom she could go, perhaps, to the odd concert which she had done rarely since Jim died. She even allowed herself to believe that if all went well and she met the right man she would consider a sexual relationship. She was certain, however, that she would never live with somebody or marry again. Now that she had become used to it, she valued the freedom that living alone gave her.

Kay thought that she just might try an ad. She alternated between thinking that Jim would have had no difficulty with her placing or answering one, and dismissing the idea from her mind altogether when she thought that some of her friends might find out. Recently the more she thought about it the more she felt she had nothing to lose. If she started the process she could keep her identity secret at the beginning and if she didn't want to proceed she could simply take the matter no further.

Kay changed her shoes at the back door and washed her hands in the utility room. She lit the fire, drew the curtains and made her evening meal. She brought it to the sitting-room and when she had finished she picked up her gardening magazine and turned to the ads. They were conveniently separated into two sections: men wanting to meet women and women wanting to meet men. There were many fewer women taking the initiative and this didn't surprise her. Kay eliminated immediately those who were well out of her age group and those who lived too far away. She thought it important that if she were to 'keep company,' and she used that old-fashioned term in her mind - it sounded respectable - he should live near enough for them to be able to meet reasonably conveniently, and far enough away to be beyond the range of any of her friends. If a man were in her age group and had not been married the question arose in her mind: 'why not?' So as far as she was concerned this was a factor that disqualified too. She had no intention at this stage of her life training someone in or coping with their problems. She wanted to spend time with somebody who was straightforward and understood the ground rules.

Kay knew that if one particular friend found out what she was doing everybody she knew would know. She was determined that this friend should not know anything of her plan, and if she did establish a relationship with a man that she would never know how she and her companion had met.

To her disappointment none of the ads met her preconditions. She was determined that she would not place her own ad; she considered this an unacceptably forward thing for a woman to do. She finished her meal, brought her tray into the kitchen and rooted out two back-numbers of the magazine. She found only one advertisement that was remotely possible.

Gentleman, south of the country, widowed six years after excellent marriage, would like to meet lady in similar circumstance to share occasional companionship and an interest in gardening.

Her imagination immediately broke loose. He was about her height, maybe an inch or two taller, round face, well-trimmed moustache, grey hair brushed flat but wavy over his ears, wore tweed suits with waistcoat, a ready smile, an acute sense of humour and a deep but gentle voice. She suddenly stopped. He might be shorter than she was, have a gormless face that seldom smiled, a scruffy beard, wear jeans and tell puerile jokes in a high squeaky voice. She laughed out loud.

Since the magazine was a back-number she thought that somebody might have already grabbed him so she answered the ad immediately and gave the minimum of information about herself; just what she considered enough to arouse his interest. When she had sealed the envelope she felt a combination of nervousness and excitement.

Just over three weeks after she had written her letter, an envelope addressed in a strange hand came through her letterbox. This was it. Her pulse quickened and she took the letter to the sitting-room and read. His name was Charles, he was in her age group, lived about thirty miles away and naturally he was a keen gardener. He enclosed a photograph. It showed him to be average height, round face, grey hair thinning and well receded at both sides. He wore a sports jacket and, she allowed, looked quite distinguished. She couldn't believe that on her first attempt she had encountered a man with whom she would have no problem being seen in public. What he might be like in private remained to be seen.

Kay thought it discreet not to reply for a week or ten days on the principle: 'keep him guessing,' and what's more he hadn't replied to her in a hurry. She wrote back, but despite being glad that Charles had sent a photograph she couldn't bring herself to send one to him. For her, photographs were personal and any photo she might have sent had particular associations for her. She felt that this venture was an entirely new development and if it worked she would be quite happy in time for their liaison to have associations and photographs of its own.

They arranged their first meeting for the foyer of a hotel roughly half way between where each of them lived. As the day approached Kay alternated between anxiety and excitement. She knew that, although she could not have had a happier marriage with Jim, the old saying was true: 'there are as good fish in the sea as ever came out of it.' In over forty years of marriage she had come to terms with all of Jim's little idiosyncrasies and irritating habits. She thought she would find it hard to do the same all over again with a new man. Then she reminded herself that Jim had had to come to terms with all of her deficiencies too. If this venture were to work Charles would have to do the same, but this was jumping the gun. Her immediate hurdle was to turn up for the assignation.

Kay chose carefully what she wore. She did not want to present too formally nor too casually. She wore her blue figured dress of fine denim material, her green coat with wraparound belt and medium heeled shoes. She drove to the hotel, making sure to arrive ten minutes late, parked, at the door took a couple of deep breaths and went in. She looked around the foyer and immediately saw Charles sitting beside a low table wearing a trench-coat. He stood up as she approached and they shook hands.

'I'm glad to see you,' he said, 'I was beginning to think you weren't coming.' They sat down.

'What would you like?'

'Tea would be good, nothing to eat, thank you.'

Their initial conversation was the traffic and the weather, but they were soon on to gardening. Each described their own garden and particular gardening interests. The conversation in the circumstances was relatively easy. After the best part of an hour with only a couple of awkward silences Charles said:

'Would you like to meet again? There's a new play on in the theatre here and it's neutral territory.'

'Thank you, I would enjoy that, but can we be clear that it's Dutch.'

'We can work that out later, but please allow me this time.'

Charles paid for the tea, they fixed a date for the theatre and he walked Kay to her car. She was greatly relieved as she drove home that there had been no embarrassment of any kind and all had gone well.

Kay had no difficulty about her plan to meet Charles again. He was none of the things that she would have found difficult, and she looked forward to their next meeting. The evening arrived and they met in the theatre foyer. They had gone beyond the handshake and hadn't yet arrived at the kiss on the cheek. Charles greeted her with:

'Hello, I've collected the tickets.' They took their seats and chatted easily before the play started and during the interval. At the end they both agreed that the play had been good. They went for one drink, which Kay insisted on buying, and leaving her at her car Charles kissed her on the cheek and said he would phone.

As she drove home Kay was happy with developments so far. Charles was considerate, interesting, had an acute sense of humour and above all he listened carefully to what she had to say.

The following week, true to his word, Charles phoned. After some small-talk Charles suggested a meal out. Kay agreed and she chose the restaurant and booked the table, but she was anxious that Charles should not see it as the cliché of the romantic candlelit dinner. It was clear to her that he didn't: they talked mainly about their past lives and about gardening and Kay arrived home having enjoyed the evening.

As the weeks and months passed Kay was more and more at ease in Charles's company. They inspected each other's gardens and had meals in each other's homes. Kay allowed that Charles was every bit as good a cook as she was, if not better. She was happy that she had done the right thing, but she was determined not to bring Charles to meet any family or friends until she was absolutely sure. She did, however, tell her sister Marjorie, whom she trusted, about Charles and how they had met. She did so primarily because, so happy was she that she thought that Marjorie, who had been widowed longer than she had been, might do the same.

Marjorie thought long and hard about it and eventually decided, like Kay, that she had nothing to lose. If she answered an ad she could pull out in the early stages without any loss of face. Unlike Kay she had no qualms about placing an ad herself. She believed it put her more in control and this is what she did. As it transpired she was less reticent about the whole process than Kay had been. She received three replies and selected the most likely amongst them. As it turned out, however, when it came to meeting the prospective companion she was infinitely more nervous than Kay had been.

The meeting was arranged for a hotel not far from where Marjorie lived. She asked Kay to go with her for moral support and a short while after she had gone in, Kay would go into the lounge and sit at a table at a distance. The day arrived and Kay drove.

When it came to it Marjorie was so nervous she almost decided not to turn up. She said to Kay:

'You've probably met the only decent available man in the county.'

But Kay reassured her that she needn't reveal her identity or take it any further if she didn't want to.

Marjorie went into the hotel and ten minutes later Kay followed. She saw Marjorie immediately over beside the window; so far, so good. She sat at a table near the door and ordered tea. Marjorie seemed to be having a fairly normal conversation, but the man had his back to Kay. She didn't like to stare but from behind he reminded her of Charles. When she had poured tea she looked again. She had no doubt in the world that the man *was* Charles.

Kay stood up and walked over to the two.

'Marje, may I introduce you to Charles?'

'Charles, this is my sister Marjorie.' With the fright Charles half stood up and fell back into his chair. He stuttered:

'There's been some mistake, I thought ………'

'Come on Marje, it's time we were gone.' Marjorie stood up and the two women marched out of the lounge. Kay looked back. Charles was still sitting there, mopping his brow with his handkerchief.

Going home in the car Kay and Marjorie alternated between anger and relief. They fumed and they laughed and decided that as they had both been lucky in love first time round they would leave it at that.

The Assault

'Mr Doherty will you please recount to the court the events of the night in question.'

'Meself an' Jemser Jordan, was walkin' home after havin' a few pints when we bumped into a couple o' birds on Camden Street. We stopped to talk to them when yer man there came over and hit me an unmerciful belt and I ended up in hospital.'

'What did you say to the girls?'

'I suppose we said "Howya girls?"'

'What happened next?'

'Yer man shouted over at us: "leave them girls alone."'

'What happened then?'

'Nuttin' happened. We was just talkin'.'

'What about your friend James?'

'Jemser done nuttin', absolutely nuttin'.'

'Did he say anything to the girls?'

'You'd want to know Jemser; talkin' to girls wouldn't be his strong suit.'

'The charge against you is one of assault……'

'Why wasn't yer man charged wid assault? You know what he done to me.'

'Why do you think he hit you?'

'He accused me of interferin' with the girls so I told him to go away and mind his own business.'

'Tell me exactly what you said.'

'Do you really want me to tell you what I said?'

'I do.'

'I said: "Fuck off and mind yer own fuckin' business or I'll knock yer fuckin' block off."'

'What happened then?'

'He came over and hit me a belt and I ended up in hospital. Jemser thought I was dead.'

'In his statement the witness claims that you hit him first and he acted in self defence.'

'O' course I hit him first, wasn't he accusing me of interferin' with the girls. Self defence? He wasn't defendin' himself against Mike Tyson.'

'I find you guilty as charged and fine you €50 and bind you to keep the peace for two years.'

'Jaysus.'

The Conservationist

The parcels' office was at the end of the platform beyond the lavatories well away from the stationmaster and the waiting-room. It was utter chaos, but there was a rationale to it known only to Matt. He had served his time there as a boy and when old 'JJ' retired he was left to run it on his own. It was over thirty years since he started and there wasn't much he didn't know about parcels in transit, but Matt considered it 'infra dig' to have to deal with passengers. When things were quiet he sat and read anything he could get his hands on.

Matt was tall and angular with wiry grey hair upon which he tried to put order by applying liberal amounts of hair oil. To the public he had an imperious manner that left no one in any doubt who was in charge. Any suggestion as to what might have happened to a missing parcel was ignored or treated with contempt by Matt. Whereas he was concerned to see that people got their parcels, he wasn't backward in making it plain that it was beyond his human capacity to give out parcels that had not arrived in his office. He considered his work beneath him and a necessary distraction in order to earn a living. His real interest in life was politics.

Matt had been bright at school, but left early to take the job at the station. He came from a big family all of whom left school as soon as work became available. When he joined the union, unlike most other young lads, he went regularly to union meetings and before he was twenty he was secretary of the branch. In due course he joined the local branch of the Labour Party, in which he had no equal for political acumen. Matt's innate intelligence and his verbal fluency, never using one word where two or more would do, led to his election to the County Council when a vacancy occurred in the so-called 'Labour seat.' He gave a good service to his constituents and made each one he dealt with feel that their problem was his personal problem and would remain so until it was solved. At Council meetings he operated on the principle that all publicity was good publicity. He said or did something outlandish at every meeting to attract the attention of the press. Over the years his increased drinking combined with his belief that most of his fellow councillors were in every way his inferiors, led to regular outbursts that were either funny or offensive, depending on the degree of his inebriation, and all were reported in the local newspaper.

One day coming back to work after lunch, Matt stopped short beside a man on the platform waiting to meet a train.

'Well, it's Paddy Maher,' he said.

'That's right,' the other replied, and then recognising Matt added, 'you're Matt Kenny'.

'So the rumour is true?' said Matt.

'It depends what the rumour is.'

'That Paddy Maher has made his fortune in England, has bought Burton Court and is coming home to litter the countryside with houses.'

'That's a fair begrudger's version of the situation,' replied Paddy.

On their first meeting after almost thirty years nothing had changed. Matt and Paddy had been far and away the two brightest boys in their class and there had been, at best, a less than friendly rivalry between them, which from time to time erupted into open hostility. Their rivalry hadn't been over academic achievement, since neither took schoolwork seriously, to the frustration of the teachers. Their rivalry was personal, and for no particular reason that anybody knew.

'And what are you up to, Matt?' asked Paddy.

'I work for the national railway network on this particular station,' replied Matt half humorously putting the best 'blas' he could on his humble job. 'May I wish you the best of luck?' Matt continued, 'and now if you'll excuse me I must get back to work.'

'Thank you,' said Paddy, and Matt, putting his newspaper under his arm with a flourish, pulled himself up to his full height and walked slowly down the platform.

The pub talk of how Paddy Maher made his money and what he was going to do with the Court was rich. The begrudgers had open season, but there were some who were full of admiration for him and believed he deserved everything he had. Matt sided with neither and would only say:

'We'll wait and see. Provided he employs union labour and pays union rates he'll have no trouble round here.'

One day Matt was putting a pile of goods from the Dublin train into his office and amongst them was a sapling with ball of earth around the roots wrapped in sacking. It was just five o'clock so he piled them up inside the door and turned the key. Next morning he began to sort the pile and saw that the weight of a heavy carton had broken the sapling. He looked at the label which said: 'Mr Patrick Maher, Burton Court' and a red sticker in capitals saying 'FRAGILE WITH CARE'. Holding the label away from him he read it again and said:

'Mr Patrick Maher, Burton Court, my backside. Paddy-with-the-arse-out-of-his-trousers Maher, School Street'd be more like it.'

Matt straightened up the tree and knew it wouldn't survive. He put it beside his stool and finished sorting the pile. He plugged in the ring, put the tea pot on it and sat down.

'Shag it,' he said under his breath. He looked at the label again and saw that the tree had come from a nursery in England. He put it out in the back room, made the tea, opened the newspaper and got on with the day.

The following afternoon a messenger from the Court arrived at the parcels office to collect the tree.

'There's no tree here for Paddy Maher,' said Matt borrowing time, and the messenger went away. Matt thought to himself:

'I have two options when they come again. Either I say it never arrived or I hand it out and say it arrived broken. Either way if he went to enough trouble he could probably prove me wrong.'

Two days later Paddy Maher landed into the parcels office.

'Good morning Patrick my old friend,' said Matt.

'I'm expecting a young tree by train and I've come to collect it,' said Paddy.

'Where was it sent from?' asked Matt, stalling.

'It's a rare specimen from a nursery in England, and I have reason to believe it's here and that you broke it,' replied Paddy.

Matt turned away from the counter and stood with his back to the fire.

'I wish to inform you,' he said, 'that what you say is absolutely true, and did your informant tell you that goods are transported by the national carrier entirely at the owner's risk and should be insured against accident.'

'And how can I be sure it was an accident?' said Paddy.

Matt went into the back room, brought out the tree and put it on the counter.

'That is an unfounded accusation Mr Maher,' said Matt, 'and as you have completed your business in this office, I suggest that you leave.'

Paddy took the tree and left.

Matt heard no more about the tree and saw Paddy Maher only rarely, in the distance, around the town. He did, however, listen carefully to every rumour that circulated about what he was doing at the Court. Matt was astute enough to glean from the stories that went round from time to time what was likely to happen. Maher was doing up the big house, which had not been occupied for some years, for himself and was planning to build a number of houses on some of the land. Matt listened to everything and said nothing. He considered it beneath the dignity of a man of his standing in the community to indulge in common gossip about someone like Paddy Maher. Once when pressed for a comment all he would say was: 'put a beggar on horseback…' which, like so many of his cryptic comments, was lost on his drinking companions. It soon became clear that there was a major renovation job under way at the Court, but that wasn't the bit Matt was waiting to hear.

One morning at work, over his cup of tea, he saw in the local newspaper what he knew would come eventually; notice of a planning application to build sixty-four houses in a townland that was part of Burton Court land. Paddy Maher had made his contacts on the local political scene and had support for his proposed development, but the conservation groups were against the plan and there was local opposition, not least by Matt himself. He kept his counsel until he saw how things developed. On the morning of the next Council meeting he went to the planning department to inspect the application. He knew enough to know that if permission were granted, one of the conservation groups would appeal. In time this was exactly what happened and the appeal was upheld. He also predicted correctly Maher's next move, a 'Section Four' application to the Council for decision by the Council members themselves that would overrule the planning department.

Matt knew that Maher's application had the support of one of the two major parties, and when he discovered that the other major party would oppose it, his blood was up, knowing it would all depend on the independents and himself. This situation arose from time to time, and Matt relished it, but on no occasion did he relish it more than this. There was much lobbying of councillors by those who supported Maher, and Matt made it plain to the first person who approached him that he hadn't made up his mind, but it would not be in Maher's interest for anybody to approach him again.

On the day of the meeting as usual Matt went to the pub before it but, in a break with custom, he had only one drink. Unusually for him he arrived at the meeting in time for the opening formalities, which was noted by the local reporters. All the councillors were present except one of the independents. The 'Section Four' application was halfway down the agenda and the pundits considered it could go either way by no more than one vote, or even by the casting vote of the chairman. The members of the press also noted that Matt was more subdued than usual and contributed once only during the early items.

During the last item before the 'Section Four' the missing independent arrived in the chamber, increasing the tension that had already begun to build. The chairman read out the application and the local representative of the political party that supported Maher, spoke glowingly about him and what a boon to the community it was that 'one of our own' should come back and in renovating Burton Court show his concern for conservation and the environment. He went on to say what a boon to the building industry in the area the proposed scheme under discussion would be. He didn't say, but implied, that if this application were not granted Mr Maher might pack his bags and go back to England. A member of the other major party described Mr Maher, in renovating the Court, as the cow that gave a good bucket of milk, but if the councillors allowed him to proceed with this development within sight of the big house, they would be helping him to kick it over. Matt chuckled.

As the debate continued it got more heated. When the independents had all spoken against the motion it became evident that it would all depend on Matt's vote, but he stuck to his seat as the councillors from the two main parties hurled invective across the chamber at each other. When the chairman was about to wind up the debate Matt stood up and addressed the chair. The reporters with pencils at the ready were waiting for some vintage Kenny and the councillors sat back ready for a long wait. With measured delivery Matt said:

'This proposed development of upmarket houses will contribute nothing to the working-class people of my constituency and so I oppose it,' and sat down. There was a cheer from the public gallery and the chairman was struck dumb in disbelief at Matt's brevity. When he had recovered he put the resolution to the meeting and it was lost by one vote.

Outside afterwards Matt was unusually reluctant to talk to reporters. He excused himself saying:

'Gentlemen, I'm sorry I can't delay, I have to go home to work on plans for a tree planting programme to enhance our local environment.'

Breganmore

Part 1

Paddy sat up on a high stool against the wall at the end of the empty bar. It was a typical country pub; a bar counter with a door and a hinged top to allow access to the back, some tables and chairs and a dart-board to one side of the turf fire. Behind the bar a display of bottles, only a few of them ever used and a photograph of a county football team from a provincial final that they lost some years ago.

Bridie emerged from the back through a curtain of multicoloured plastic strips.

'Howya Paddy?'

'Howya Bridie?'

She took a glass from the shelf above the bar and held it under the tap. She pulled the lever slowly, released it and left the stout to settle.

'Things are quiet to-night,' Paddy said.

'Quiet is right, not a sinner only yourself.'

Paddy took out a cigarette and lit it. 'It's that bloody carry on in Breganmore. People are gullible when they'll believe that kind of thing.'

'A few years ago people saw the statue move in Ballinspittle,' said Bridie, 'and that was more than a handful of auld women. There was even a Protestant journalist from Dublin saw it move.'

Paddy flicked his cigarette into the big glass ashtray on the counter. 'But the priests didn't believe it, and no bishop went next nigh or near it.'

'The priests are taking an interest this time.'

'But they're not saying one way or the other. They're keeping their options open and delighted to see the people packing the churches again.'

'I hear they're putting on extra confessions more places than Breganmore. There's people going to confession that haven't been in a box for years.'

Though never having given the second coming any thought before, since the rumours began everybody in the district had become an expert on the subject.

'How, in the name of God,' said Paddy, 'could anyone in their right mind believe that a man in a cottage up the hills above Breganmore could be the second coming of Christ?'

Recent events had begun to make Breganmore even more famous than Ballinspittle. People were saying that in Ballinspittle it was the mother, but in Breganmore it was Himself and that Ballinspittle was the warning that wasn't taken.

'What they're saying,' said Bridie, taking the head off the pint, topping it up and putting it in front of Paddy, 'is that it had to happen sooner or later, isn't it in the Bible. With the state the world is in, isn't it a good time to happen, and why not here in one of the last countries in the world where Catholics still practise their religion?'

'Well he's only just in time. There are less and less practising it. More and more are choosing the bits they like and dispensing with the bits they don't.'

'At least they're Catholics of one sort or another,' she said, 'even if they are bad ones. What's he going to do about Protestants for God's sake; there's a variety of them for every day of the year.'

'Wouldn't it be gas if it turned out that they were right and we were wrong.'

'They can't be right. Wasn't it dinned into us in school that the Catholic Church is the one true Church, and so they must all be wrong. Weren't we taught that unless you were a Catholic you were going to hell, and weren't we all sorry for the Protestants, for some of them are fine decent people.'

'I don't think that's the case now. The Council changed all that.'

'What's the Council got to do with it?' Bridie asked.

'Not the County Council, for God's sake, the Vatican Council. They're now our separated brothers and sisters and we have 'uconimical' services and all, so they can't be that bad.'

'It's a big change from the days we couldn't go into their churches even for the funeral of a neighbour.'

'Well tell me this, what about the millions of Buddhists and Mahommedans, and fellas like that? What's going to happen to them?' asked Paddy.

'According to what we were taught not only are they not Catholics, they're not even Christians, so they've no chance.'

'A terrible waste of people if you ask me. If you were God would you manufacture millions and millions of people knowing for certain they were all going to hell?'

'Isn't that what missionaries are for?'

'Well they're making heavy weather of it aren't they?' said Paddy, and after a pause added, 'for Jesus' sake don't be annoying me. It'd be a great deal easier if he overlooked the apple incident and left us all in the garden; you'd have none of this kind o' carry on to-day.'

'Things weren't as quiet as this when the breathalyser came in,' said Bridie.

'There's a big difference between losing your licence and losing your soul.'

Johnny, Bridie's husband, came into the bar from the back to see the state of play.

'Howya Paddy?'

'Howya Johnny? The whole countryside is at mass in Bregan.'

'They're taking it very serious, aren't they?'

'That's because the priests aren't ruling it out. They won't give a straight answer one way or the other.'

'Even if they did, wouldn't the holy Joes know better. The country is full of pious people that know better than the priests.'

'It's hard to know what the priests know, but they don't know as much as they knew years ago, at least if they do they're not telling. Years ago the priests told you in simple language what you had to do to save your soul, but to-day they can't give you a straight answer to anything, and then they tell you to follow your conscience. They're gone like the Protestants: make up your own mind.'

Paddy nodded towards his almost empty glass and Bridie put a clean glass under the tap and pulled the lever. Johnny continued:

'They say that a good number of the priests have women one way or the other.' 'Casey was just the tip of the iceberg,' said Paddy.

'Casey was no iceberg.'

'You know what I mean.'

'Indeed I do, sure don't you remember Father Hayes in Tourneenbeg?'

'Isn't it a terrible thing to deprive a man of filling his basic instinct, priest or not.'

'Bregan will deprive people of more than their basic instincts. I hear some people are afraid of their lives; the end of the world and judgement and hell staring them in the face.'

'For God's'sake don't be annoying me; people are gullible or ignorant or maybe both; how in the name of God could a man in a cottage up the hills be the second coming of Christ. If there's going to be such a thing isn't he supposed to come on clouds with angels and trumpets and all that class o' thing.'

'Do you not believe there'll be a second coming?' Johnny asked.

'To be honest with you Johnny I don't know what the hell I believe. The whole feckin' thing is so hard to believe, sometimes I believe nothin'.

'Well there's your brother,' said Bridie, 'but he wouldn't want his customers to know for fear he'd go out of business.'

'That's not true,' said Johnny, 'I don't believe nothing, I just have my own way of believing.' He put the pint on the counter and took the empty glass.

'Well then you're a Protestant,' said Paddy, as he counted out the price of the pint.

'You know very well I'm not, it's just there are some things it's hard to believe.'

'Like the second coming of Christ? Well if you don't believe it you're not a proper Catholic. You either believe what the Church teaches or you don't. It's as simple as that. Who gave you licence to think for yourself?' Paddy goaded, wiping froth off his upper lip.

'Oh he thinks for himself all right,' said Bridie.

'It's the foolish man that doesn't, whatever the Church tells you,' said Johnny.

'Sure the Church has an infallible Pope and a regiment of cardinals; what's a publican that left school at fourteen against that?' Paddy provoked again:

'He's a man with a right to make up his own mind. How can the Church expect you to believe something you don't believe?'

'I agree with that, but a priest would tell you you'd need to inform yourself before you made up your mind.'

'Sure you could spend the rest of your life informing yourself,' Johnny came back, 'and still not be at the end of it. I'm happy enough with the information I have to know what I believe and what I don't, and to be honest I don't believe the half it.'

'Begod then Johnny aren't you the fierce sceptical man, and I'd never have guessed it. I thought I was the only doubter around Breganmore. So if you don't believe the half the Church teaches, you hardly have much time for what's going on in Bregan?'

'No time at all for it.'

'However,' Bridie joined in, 'if it turns out to be true we'll all have a bit of an advantage since we're all named after saints that'll put in a word for us.'

'Well if that's the case it'll leave some fellas in Spain that are called after Jesus himself in a strong position; he'll surely go easy on his own,' said Paddy.

'His own are the Jews, and it'll be a good one to see what he does about them after what they did to him,' came back Johnny.

'Why don't we do that here?' asked Paddy.

'What, crucify the fella' in Bregan?' said Bridie.

'No, christen boys *Jesus*, don't we christen girls *Mary*.'

'It's all right with those Spanish names,' said Paddy, 'but it wouldn't go with Irish names; Jesus O'Meara. Think of fellas calling the barman to order a drink; "Jesus, a pint and a Gold Label," or a fella up in court with the judge saying: "Jesus Murphy, I find you guilty of drunk and disorderly conduct and sentence you to six months in prison."' Johnny looked at Bridie and wiped the grin off his face and said to his only customer:

'Paddy you're a terrible man.'

'Sure that's the way it'd be; you couldn't be sure how the baby was going to turn out when he grew up.'

The door of the bar opened and a carload of men arrived into the bar after mass at Breganmore. At first there was polite conversation and then Paddy opened up:

'Any news of your man?'

'Who's that now?' inquired one of the newcomers.

'Your man in the cottage above Bregan.'

'Not a word.'

'He didn't turn up at mass?'

'Not that I know.'

'That'd be a queer one. If he went to communion, he'd be eatin' himself.'

'Now Paddy,' said Johnny, afraid his customers would take offence.

'Well it's true. If he is Christ and he goes to communion, what else would he be doin'. Maybe he goes to the Protestant church where he wouldn't have to do that.'

There was silence while the company absorbed Paddy's theological point.

'I hear some of the women stay on for extra devotions until the priest has to sweep them out to close the church; like Johnny here on a Saturday night.'

'One way or the other a bit more religion can do no harm, isn't the country gone to the dogs,' said Bridie.

'If in doubt hedge your bets,' said Paddy.

Johnny was sorry he had shown his hand to Paddy for fear he might draw him into discussion in front of customers. He was afraid he was going to provoke a row, so as he wiped the counter he said casually: 'With the bit of fine weather the land'll dry up in no time.'

Part 2

Father Mahon, the parish priest of Breganmore, back from evening mass sank into his comfortable, well-worn armchair in the study, drew the stool in and put his feet up. He was exhausted from the extra confessions and masses he had to put on to satisfy public demand.

He was due to retire in a year and for the last couple of years he had been ticking over, doing no more than saying mass, baptising, marrying and burying and a few more essentials, simply because he hadn't the energy. Then this whole business blew up at the worst possible time, and to make things worse he hadn't a curate and there was no immediate sign of getting one.

He hadn't had time to give much thought to the matter of the stranger, but no matter who he was it could only be good that people were filling the church. As far as he was concerned there was another bonus from the whole affair; the giving to the collections had increased three or fourfold. It was much more than an increase from the extra attenders at mass; there were as many notes as coin and he had had to get special baskets that were deep enough to stop notes falling off. If things kept going the way they were, there was a good chance he would have the debt for the renovations to the church paid off before he retired.

Norah knocked on the door and came in. She carried a small tray with a jug of water, a glass and a plate of ham sandwiches. She pulled over the small table and placed the tray beside Father Mahon.

'Another good crowd tonight, Father.'

She always used 'Father' on first addressing the priest, but didn't repeat it during the rest of a conversation until the end. She hated the way people used it after every sentence; she was determined not to be obsequious. Neither was she casual with Father Mahon, for whom she had been housekeeper since he came to the parish. She had a high regard for him and treated him as a man whose office deserved respect, but none the less was flesh and blood like everyone else. As far as he was concerned she hit just the right note, and he had great confidence in her.

'No matter what, it has to be good. It's like the old days, but with so many receiving communion it takes longer, and I'm not getting any younger.'

Norah reached for the bottle of Gold Label from the cupboard over the priest's desk and put it on the tray.

'Sure there's none of us doing that.'

'Norah, tell me the truth, what do you make of the whole business?' the priest asked as he unscrewed the cap of the bottle and poured some whiskey. He sometimes asked her opinion when he wanted to hear what was being said in the parish.

'I don't know what to think. You'd have a better chance of knowing what to make of it than I would.'

'Well, despite what lay people think, priests haven't privileged information, and it's years since I turned anyone into a goat.'

They both laughed.

'To be serious, since you preached the sermon two Sundays ago saying wait and see, you lost the ear of a good number of pious people. For some reason many of them have a fierce need to believe that the end is near.'

'What else can I do but tell them to wait and see; the Church has been around too long to make the mistake of rushing its fences. I suppose it'll be like Ballinspittle, it'll wear off in its own time, without the Church saying one way or the other.'

'That's what the people are saying, that the Church is sitting on the fence.'

The priest did not respond.

'Good night, Father,' Norah said, and closed the study door behind her.

Father Mahon woke in his chair to a loud knocking on the hall door, followed by a persistent ring on the bell. He waited, but the knocking and ringing continued. He heard Norah coming up the hall from the kitchen. She normally answered the door and filtered callers or took messages; she had learned discretion in protecting Father Mahon from nuisance calls. She put the security chain in place and asked through the closed door:

'Who's is it?'

'Don't mind who it is. Open the fucking door.'

'What do you want?'

'I want to talk to the priest.'

'What about?'

'About the wife.'

At that moment Father Mahon arrived into the hall.

'Who is it?'

'What's your name?' Norah shouted through the door.

'Paudge Heafy.'

'It's Paudge Heafy, he says he wants to talk to you about his wife. He sounds as if he's drunk.'

'Let him in.'

'I'll let you in,' said Norah, 'if you'll stop the bad language.'

'What fucking bad language? Will you open the fucking door.'

The priest signalled to Norah to go back to the kitchen, took the chain off and opened the door. His large black form filled the opening and he looked down on the dishevelled figure of Paudge Heafy, standing on the step.

'Good night, Father, have you got a minute?'

'What's it about?'

'It's about the wife.'

'What about your wife?'

Paudge looked behind him both ways.

'It's not the kind of thing I can discuss in public, Father.'

'Can it wait till to-morrow?'

'Begod it can't Father, because it'll happen again to-night.'

Father Mahon stood back and Paudge Heafy swayed into the hall. The priest shut the door, led the way into the study and pulled out a chair and told his parishioner to sit down. He sat back into his own chair and asked:

'Now what is it that'll happen again to-night?'

Paddy Heafy rooted in his pocket and pulled out a packet of cigarettes.

'Do you mind if I smoke, Father?'

'No,' Father Mahon said abruptly, starting to lose patience.

Paddy focussed on the priest with a puzzled look on his face.

'Do you mean, Father, no you don't mind or no I can't smoke?'

'Get to the point,' said the priest.

'Well Father, when a man gets married isn't it true to say that he has what's called conjugal rights?'

The priest made no response and waited. Paudge continued:

'Well Father, since all this carry on about your man up the hills, me wife is denying me me conjugal rights, and as far as I'm concerned that's against me religion.'

Father Mahon said nothing. Paudge Heafy sat forward on his chair.

'Father, she thinks the end of the world is comin' and she wants to keep herself in good condition for the big day.'

'What big day are you talking about?'

'The last judgement, Father, but I keep telling her it's a sin to deny her lawful married husband his conjugal rights and it's nothing but her Christian duty to grant them. Am I not right Father? She's not keeping herself pure at all, she's acting against her religion.'

'And is that what you came here to ask me?'

'Yes Father, I knew that if I could go home and tell her you said it was all right the job'd be oxo.'

'I'll tell you no such thing.'

Father Mahon stood up, went to the study door and opened it. Paudge Heafy rose, steadied himself and followed the priest into the hall.

'Well, there's nothing for it now Father but the law. You can't deny a man his conjugal rights, second coming or no second coming. Good night now.'

Father Mahon held the hall door open, and Paudge Heafy left with a cigarette already in his mouth.

The priest went back into his study and sat down. He began to reflect on people's attitude to the man in the cottage. He wondered how the whole thing started. Why were some people so credulous? What was this great need for the miraculous? Were they people whose lives were so intolerable that they wanted them to be over? Or did they want some kind of assurance that an ordinary faith didn't give. How in the name of God could they believe that a kind of hippie in a cottage up the hills was Christ's second coming? But then nobody ever told them much about the second coming, and come to think of it he had never thought much about it himself. What exactly is Church teaching on the subject, he began to ask himself.

He sat back into his chair, put his feet up and began to feel again what he had felt on and off over the last couple of years: that he would be glad to retire. He thought of his own time as a young curate when everything was straightforward; the Church taught and the people believed. He had no doubt that people were happier. It was true what old people said, that people had fewer material things and less comfort and convenience, but they were more contented. Right enough most of them were ignorant, he didn't like using the word and wouldn't to anyone else, but it was true. They were less well-educated and more superstitious. But what had all this education done for people. It had turned some of them scepticism and disbelief. Even some of the most sophisticated and educated people had learned nothing more than the catechism, and perhaps had forgotten most of that, so when they were confronted with a theological matter they hadn't the tools. They lived in the modern world with television and newspapers and nothing was exempt from scrutiny. Even the simplest people had grounds for doubts and the Church still treated them like children.

The very idea that he was suggesting that lay people should be educated in theology surprised him. But the more he thought the more he became aware that that was part of the problem; people were educated to think critically in every area of life except belief. So when some people applied the criteria of science and other disciplines to their faith and the Church they were both found wanting. Some people, however, when confronted with the problem of belief in the modern world retreated into a literal and simplistic acceptance of Church teaching, while others looked for the intervention of God through the miraculous to confirm their faith and reassure them in the face of questioning and doubt.

Father Mahon had never taken the trouble to put all this together before. He had always had doubts himself, but never much time to pursue them. He kept himself informed theologically and had been excited by the Vatican Council, but much of that seemed to have been overruled. Now he was tired and wanted a bit of peace. He had constructed a belief system of his own, but publicly he more or less held the official line. He couldn't bring himself to cope with the problems that sharing his own thoughts with his people would bring. In fact if he told them the half of what he believed, he might be removed and banished to some convent chaplaincy until he was back on the rails.

For the second time that evening Father Mahon dozed off and when he woke from a deep sleep it was a quarter to two. He eased himself out of his chair, turned out the lights and went to bed.

Part 3

For some weeks now the local press had been reporting events in and around Breganmore; the vigils in the local church, the return to confession and the extra masses. A reporter approached the man in his cottage for an interview, but he declined politely and closed the door. The reporter called again but there was no reply. The national papers had just begun to report the affair but with no great enthusiasm, and it was mentioned on a phone-in programme on radio.

As with most controversies there were people with opinions both ways, and a fair proportion that had no opinion at all. The more-than-averagely religious took the affair seriously. The majority were not sure what to make of it, but were largely doubtful and there were those who thought the whole thing was ridiculous, some of whom simply ignored events and some who were vociferous in condemning the whole affair as primitive superstition.

Rumours circulated freely. The most common rumours were about miraculous cures. People were said to be throwing away crutches and others were said to be cured of cancer and a host of other illnesses. When a reporter from one of the national papers came to look for interviews he couldn't find anyone that would admit to being cured, only a local sceptic who asked: 'What's the point of being cured if you believe the end is here anyway?' Word went around that the end would come forty days after the stranger came, but no one could be sure exactly which day that was since nobody saw him arrive.

People were coming from all over the country to the devotions in the church in Breganmore. Coaches blocked the village street, and the Guards had to ask a farmer to give a field for parking. The two village shops were doing a fine business and traders in the neighbouring towns felt the benefits. Business in the pubs was not affected except for coach drivers looking for tea and sandwiches.

Father Mahon was at the end of his tether and applied to the bishop for help, but the bishop would not send a priest, even temporarily, lest it would be seen as approval. Father Mahon told the bishop that he hadn't given his approval to the people but he still had to provide masses for the crowds that came, so the bishop agreed to commission two extra lay ministers of the eucharist, without training.

In a few weeks local and national press coverage dwindled significantly, but the devotion of the pious did not. There was, however, a trickle of foreign reporters to be seen around Breganmore. This gave encouragement to the devout, who saw the interest of the foreign press as the beginning of making the event universal. The foreign press, however had another view. They saw the whole affair as a curious phenomenon of peasant religion, like other similar superstitious instances around the world. They were asking questions like: how come such happenings as this and Ballinspittle only happened to Roman Catholics? But the pious replied: 'Because the Roman Catholic Church is the one true

Church of God and is the only religion that has the whole truth, and isn't it natural that God will deal with the world through his own.'

'How come then,' the reporters asked, 'that he didn't land in Rome, why Breganmore?'

'Who are we to question the ways of God?' the pious replied.

By this time the devout had set up a twenty-four hour vigil in the field opposite the cottage. They made a little altar on which they put a picture of Jesus that they claimed had a great likeness of the man, and said the rosary in shifts throughout the day.

The reporters tried to interview Father Mahon, but with the help of Norah he avoided them for a long time. Eventually a reporter cornered him one evening leaving the church after mass.

'Father, what's your opinion of the whole affair?'

'What affair?'

'The second coming.'

'What second coming?'

'The man in the cottage.'

'My opinion doesn't matter.'

'Have you discussed it with your bishop?'

'No.'

'Do you know what he thinks?'

'No.'

'Well how can we know what the Church thinks?'

'The Church hasn't an opinion on the matter.'

'What about the Pope? Has he said anything? Surely when the second coming happens he'll know if it's the real thing or not.'

'I'm sure the Pope hasn't ever heard of Breganmore, let alone know what's going on here.'

'If you're that sure it's not the real thing why don't you tell people?'

'Anything that brings the people back to prayer and devotion must be good.'

'Even if it's not true?'

Father Mahon was becoming impatient but knew that the worst thing he could do was to show it. He wasn't used to being challenged in this way. Even the Irish reporters had a little more respect than this.

'Well gentlemen, I must go.'

He turned and went back into the church.

Soon after this, interest in the second coming began to wane. The press had milked the story for all it was worth but the pious kept up their vigil. Father Mahon still held the extra masses and confessions, but the numbers had fallen off. Things were beginning to return to normal in Breganmore when it happened.

One evening there were loud rumblings in the distance. The pious knew exactly what it was and rushed to the church. Bright flashes were seen in the sky on the horizon. The weather became increasingly close and oppressive.

In the small hours of the morning loud claps of thunder woke the whole countryside and lightning lit up every house in the village. There followed the most almighty thunderstorm that seemed to go on for ever. People lay terrified in their beds. People prayed who hadn't said a prayer for years. Apart from the lightning the village was in total darkness. The thunder became louder and the lightning more frequent. Thunder and lightning seemed to be happening at the same time when an almighty rushing sound drowned out the thunder as a cloudburst descended, hammering on roofs and flowing over gutters and downpipes. The rain collapsed the makeshift shelter of the members of the rosary rota opposite the cottage. They were petrified and abandoned their vigil. In their dash for home they were soaked to the skin. In no time there was a foot of water on the main street and flowing into houses.

Slowly the storm abated. Still people were afraid to move but by half-past six or seven most people had surveyed the damage. By nine o'clock the skies began to clear and the sun broke through. Members of the rosary vigil returned to re-erect their shelter and discovered the front door of the cottage open. They approached tentatively and called into the hall:

'Hello! Are you there?'

There was no reply. Some of the women ventured into the kitchen. There was a milk carton, a half pan of sliced bread and some dirty dishes on the table. It was clear that the man had gone.

They went back into the village and told their friends. They had no idea what to say or think. Word spread around the village. Some people went out to the cottage to look. There was no doubt that the man was no longer there.

For weeks there were rumours of sightings but slowly the village returned to normal. The bus tours stopped, the journalists disappeared, Father Mahon took off the extra masses and the bishop decommissioned the untrained lay ministers of the eucharist.

About the Author

Patrick Semple is a former Church of Ireland clergyman. Patrick has had two volumes of memoirs published, and two collections of poems. He was editor of 'A Parish Adult Education Handbook,' and ghost wrote 'That Could Never Be,' a memoir by Kevin Dalton. He has had short stories published and broadcast. His novel 'Transient Beings' was published in 2012 followed by his travelogue 'Curious Cargo'. His creative writing guide 'Being Published' was published in 2013.

Patrick teaches a creative writing course at the National University of Ireland Maynooth, Adult Education Department and for four years has done public readings of his work in Kempten, Bavaria.

He has a website at ***www.patricksemple.ie***

OTHER BOOKS BY PATRICK SEMPLE

TRANSIENT BEINGS
A novel

Some transient beings come from the past and pass through the present and some in the present refuse to leave the past. How long will the idyllic rectory in the heart of rural Ireland in the 1970s hide the secrets of those who live behind its walls?

'There is no greater heresy than that the office sanctifies the holder of it.' and this is as true for the rector's wife as it is for the rector.

CURIOUS CARGO
A travelogue

This is an account of voyages taken by Patrick and his wife Hilary on cargo vessels carrying everything from bananas to buses. It is the kind of travelling the world thinks has passed into folklore. Midnight coffee on the bridge with the captain; weeks at sea between ports; colour, culture and novelty when you put to shore. There are storms and placid sunlit seas. There is the sound of the ocean and all the while *"the machine is machining"*.

BEING PUBLISHED
A creative-writing guide

A dispatch from the front lines of writing and a personal account of Patrick Semple's inspiration for writing and how he came to be published. It is also Patrick's distillation of the principles of the craft of writing. It is based on the creative writing he teaches at the National University of Ireland, Maynooth.

Lightning Source UK Ltd.
Milton Keynes UK
UKOW04f1313240913

217813UK00001B/10/P